Dancing Nightmares

Autumn Augustus

Published By
SickFace Music
January 2017

Dancing Nightmares by
Autumn A. Augustus

Copyright © 2010 Autumn A. Augustus
ALL RIGHTS RESERVED

First Printing – December 2010
ISBN: 978-1-60047-522-1
Wasteland Press, Shelbyville, KY
www.wastelandpress.net

NO PART OF THIS BOOK MAY BE REPRODUCED IN ANY FORM, BY
PHOTOCOPYING OR BY ANY ELECTRONIC OR MECHANICAL
MEANS, INCLUDING INFORMATION STORAGE OR RETRIEVAL SYSTEMS, WITHOUT PERMISSION IN WRITING FROM THE COPYRIGHT OWNER/AUTHOR

Printed in the U.S.A.

This book is dedicated to Veronica Venus Verve and Slade Neighbors, the only members of my family who have ever believed in me. Thank you for being there to validate my arts!

Also to the many alumni of Cirkus Pandemonium who have shared many beautiful stages and dreams with me on our journeys through life.

Table of Contents

Not All Who Wander Are Lost	4
For Love of the Darker Side	5
The Time Shop	7
Melancholia	14
The Dark Woods	16
The Dark Woods Song	20
Gods We Are	22
This is a living soul!	30
How I Got Dreadlocks	31
Fairy Cocoon	43
The Bear and the Mountain	45
Meet Me at the Spot	54
The Show Must Go On	55
Cirkus Theme Song	71
Cemetery Demons	72
The Portal Tree	102
Weeping Willows	102
Dance of the Banshees	104
Wings of Night	119
The Gods Down There	121
Garden Of Star Lilies	155
Dancing Nightmares	158
Passages of My Mind	175
About the Author	177

Not All Who Wander Are Lost

Not   The destination
But the journey.

All
  Who come may
  Play a part.
  Who   Knows the
way   The get to
the show?

Wander
  About then   To and fro.

Are   We here or
Are we there?

Lost
  Is a nice place   To be.

For Love of the Darker Side

For Reasons that could not be intellectually explained.

Love brings out my passions for what is not thought

Of as tangible or even real.
Out there, lurking in

The shadows of the city and in secret groves,

Darker spirits loom to twist and bind the

Side of yourself known only to the Gods.

The Time Shop

"Stop"

"Close your eyes. Open your hand.

"Hold on just a second now, I almost...have...it. Yes!

"Now, now don't move or you might just lose it see. I'm going to put it in your hand but you have to very careful here see.

"Ahhh! There we are, yes!

"Ok, ok, you can open your eyes now. But slowly, Slowly!" I opened my eyes and looked at the old man.

"Well! He said and gestured to my open palm. I looked at my hand and saw nothing and told him so.

"Look closer." He placed my hand two inches from my eyes and there it was.

There on my hand was a tiny fleck of sand. Not just any kind of sand mind you, this fleck of sand was purple and I could feel it tingle on my hand as it sat there.

"Do you see it?"

I breathed the word yes as I saw the world in front of me swim away as I was transported into a realm of my existence alone.

"It's strange how one scarcely notices things even when one passes by every day on the way to work and school. For I could swear that I had never seen this strange shop I was standing in until that one day. The fateful day that I decided to walk inside the time shop and get the broken watch I had carried around in my pocket for weeks fixed. It had been an heirloom from my grandfather and I had received it the winter before.

I had never been in there before and had heard of it only once from a colleague of mine who told me about the man that owned the store. He had told me that he was a great professor of math and science and also an excellent watchmaker. The store was between a bakery and a pawnshop and seemed to be crammed into a very small space indeed. The front of the store was nondescript with a brick wall and a heavy wooden door above which were the words "The Time Shop". The space between the two surrounding stores was narrow and dirty with whitewash on the bricks covering old graffiti.

When I walked in however the store looked huge! The floor was covered in faded hard wood, and the air seemed thick with tiny floating particles of dust, so dense it made the bright lights overhead seem dim. The walls around me were covered from floor to ceiling with shelves thickly packed with books and odd trinkets and knickknacks. Including many varied and beautiful watches and time pieces of astounding detail. Hanging from the ceiling were more clocks and odd hangings that gave one a claustrophobic feeling even though the end of the hall was beyond sight.

I was looking at the various knickknacks on the shelf when a curious man entered the room. He had a small head of graying hair, and little round glasses that horrifically magnified his beady little eyes. He walked over to me with a gait that suggested that one leg was slightly shorter than the other. When he saw me, a twinkle appeared in his eyes and a huge grin overtook his previously gloomy countenance.

"Yes, can I help you?" He asked with a slightly squeaky voice.

"Yeah, um, I was wondering if you could fix this." I said as I pulled out the antique pocket watch. It was made of fine silver overlaid with a delicate plate of gold in the design of an alchemist in his study reading a big scroll. The cover snapped open to reveal a watch face of mother of pearl, the numbers and the hands made of gold also. An exemplary watch, I should have known better than to show it off or get it fixed but I was extremely curious about it and wanted to get it appraised and know more about it if possible. The look on the old watchmaker's eyes told me that he had seen this watch before and that there was more to its history than I had first expected.

"Where on earth did you get this?" He asked in a gasp.

"It was an heirloom from my grandfather, he treasured it much in life and gave it to me in his will. He passed away last winter. "Was your grandfather Ardus Brooks?" He asked with a sly intonation.

"Why, yes! You knew him?"

"Ah! At last you came!" He exclaimed and grasped my shoulders in a great bear hug I would not think possible from such a mouse of a man. "I've been waiting for you to show up you know.

"He was a teacher of mine actually, I heard he lost his mind a while back but in his prime he taught me to really see the world for what it is."

"And what's that?" I asked with curiosity.

"Well, I can't explain it all at once, but here make yourself comfortable, yes..." He turned around and cleared a small amount of working space on the table and gestured me to set my belongings down. I did, as all I had in hand were my textbooks from college. I set my books upon the counter next to me and was startled when the old man cackled as he picked up my calculus book.

I looked at him and chuckled out of surprise and asked him what was so funny. "This book," He said as he thumbed through it then slapped the cover shut and threw it into a large green garbage bin.

"Hey!" I cried. "What's the big idea?" I reached for my book but he laughed and blocked my way.

"You don't need such foolishness." He said. "Look, I'll show you how. He pulled out a piece of paper from nowhere and plucked a pen out from behind my ear. "Let me show you how it's really done."

Upon a large piece of paper, and began to frantically write down numbers and mumble to himself. He paused for a moment with a startle as if realizing that I was standing behind him. "Ok, here's what is wrong with all this crap you've been studying. You see they were mostly close but I've seen those books before and their missing a few key things…" He began to go off scribbling more numbers and arcane symbols upon the paper until I feared losing his point.

"Hold on just a second," I said as I was barley grasping his point. "Just how do you know that this is the right answer and the others are wrong?"

"How do I know this?" He asked, and chuckled to himself. "Well that is an answer that we shall see if you deserve. Now pay attention." He walked through some crazy equations that touched upon the theories I already knew but involved boggling complex formulas about relativity and time. Every now and then he would pause and make sure I was understanding him and making me relay what he was showing me. Incredibly I was grasping this for the most part.

"Well yes, I'm not actually sure about what you meant about influential matter. Could you explain more about this theory?"

"Ha, ha!" I knew you would be the one to get it!" The little man's eyes exploded with joy as he jumped up and down. "You don't know how long I have waited for you to walk through those doors. You see, old Ardus and I were working on this theory for a long time until his mind went out on him. I finished the developments on it since then and have been waiting for someone to share it with. Influential matter is the stuff the Gods use. It's like how they move and create without actually being there!"

"And you said you've figured it out? Have you tried it?"

"Oh, yeah! Let me show you. Wait here."

"Stop." He said as he abruptly turned around. Almost as if he were talking to himself.

"Close your eyes. Open your hand." I did as I was told and he grasped my hand and turned it palm up. I then heard him scurry off. "Hold on just a second now." I heard a few things fall and break as he rustled about the room. I was tempted to peek but didn't dare to. "I almost (Bump) Have (Crash!) it (Clonk!) Yes!

"Now, now don't move or you might just lose it see." Of course, I couldn't see because my eyes were shut. "I'm going to put it in your hand, but you have to be very careful here see." I felt his hand once again enclose mine, and a slight electric feeling that I couldn't quite define.

"Ahhh! There we are, yes!" I felt and heard him step back and once again crash into something behind him.

"Ok, ok. You can open your eyes now. But slowly, Slowly!"

I opened my eyes and looked at the old man. His wild white hair framing his pale spectacled face that was gleaming with pleasure.

"Well!" he said and gestured to my open palm. I looked at my hand and saw nothing and told him so.

The old man chuckled and whispered. "Look closer." He then shoved my hand not two inches away from my eyes, and there it was...

There on my hand was a tiny fleck of sand. Not just any king of sand however. This fleck of sand was more dazzling than any jewel I had ever seen. It was purple and I could feel it tingle on my hand as it sat there and it was radiating shimmering light.

"Do you see it?" He whispered.

I breathed the word yes as I became absorbed into the sight of the tiny jewel and the world was swimming away from me and a new world came into view. I was transported to a new realm that put my singular existence alone in front of God's.

I seemed to be inside the workings of a very large and intricate clock. My surroundings were huge and I could not see any walls or borders, the clutter of the shop I had just been standing in was replaced by a multitude of changing scenes around me. As I watched around me, I began to see important scenes of my life imprinted upon the wheels and turnings of an enormous clock. Here was my childhood playground occupied by the screaming children I hadn't seen since I had grown up. The next scene was with my parents and I as a small child, it seemed we were reading a child's book. I began to flit from scene to scene when I saw the stack of math books. Suddenly the equations that the old man had been showing mere began to fly across my vision at a rapid pace. I was stricken as I realized that I was beginning to understand everything that had to do with the subject and my realm of knowledge was vast!

I turned from that scene and behind me was another stack of books and as I opened one, I was fed the thoughts and theories of the great ancient philosophers. The knowledge open to me was infinite; I only had to walk to a different part of this intricate maze of time and the answers to the great questions were laid open to me. The clock I stood in was composed of hundreds no thousands of gears and realms each with its own subjects and developments of thought and matter. I ran past the few scenes of my life that stood before me and into the past before I was born. I found myself witnessing the trials of the great depression of the early 19th century. I understood the labors and hardships of those that had lived through those trying times. As I looked past, I saw the workings of great machines becoming born to the industrial revolution.

In a great rush of revelation, I began to run from cog to cog of this giant clock I was inside. Striving to know everything ever known to man for as I touched my hand to a great wheel, my head was filled with understanding. Suddenly I stumbled perhaps on the wheel beneath me or on something from The Time Shop's threshold. As I fell, I saw this wonderful world that I had just discovered slowly disappearing before me, then I found myself face down on the sidewalk in front of The Time Shop I had entered ages ago. It seemed I had dropped my precious grain of a gem in my fall.

I found myself the center of attention of a large crowd inquiring of my well-being. The old mousy man who had given me that grain of sand helped me to my unsteady feet. I asked him what had happened and he said I seemed to have fallen over a crack in the sidewalk. I told him he was right about everything he had taught me and I was greeted by a puzzled look.

"Why son, I think you must have hit your head on your fall. What are you talking about?" I only nodded my head in confusion. "Let's get you to the hospital." He said.

I mumbled something about being ok and stumbled though the growing crowd that parted for me in silence. I wandered aimlessly reviewing the awesome equations in my head when I was picked up by a police officer sometime in the night. The nice man escorted me to a homeless shelter while I tried to explain to the officer what I had experienced, but he only took me for a mindless vagrant with no place to go. At the shelter, they bandaged my bleeding head and gave me a place to rest in troubled sleep.

The next day I returned to The Time Shop to speak to the old man. When I found the street again and located the bakery, my heart skipped a beat. I hustled down the street to fine an abandoned shop with a boarded-up door and nothing more. I walked further down the street to the pawnshop and asked the owner about The Time Shop. I faltered when I saw the old man from the day before only he looked different, cleaner, and younger... He recognized me only as the poor soul who fell in the street yesterday. I finally blurted out. "But where is The Time Shop?" He told me that there had once been a clock shop next door but it had been boarded up years ago, after the owner had gone insane. He started to tell me more but then a man ran out the door with some stolen goods and he ran down the street after him.

I stumbled out of the shop and searched the gutter for my piece of glorious sand that I knew was there somewhere. I knew it was there somewhere and I only had to find it before I became once again the most powerful person in the world with all the knowledge right there at my fingertips. Frantically I picked through the dirt and debris until the owner of the bakery had me chased off by the cops.

I was picked up by the same police officer as the night before. "Come on you," He said "let's go." I followed him again to the homeless shelter because I couldn't for the life of me remember where I lived or what I had done with my wallet or my name. I hated it at the shelter though; it was filled with crazy men and women who were lost in the world. I just couldn't relate to them.

The next day I returned to the same street and searched the gutter for my precious jewel.

Melancholia

The heavy eyes of tear ridden moments. Melancholia
embraces my being and I Am drowning in the waves of
now.
The fires of destruction only last so long,
Yet the ashes remain like scars that have
Bleed mightily and sorely, festering breaches Steaming while
the skin of time reaches, to cover the evidence of pain.

Perhaps it will become a field of flowers, open
And accepting of the blackened frame that lies in
Testimony. Or perhaps even you will build a New factory atop the
old, like a new garment
Meant to hide a hideous mark upon the body.

Underneath however, the soil still screams
From pain in memory of the boiling touch

Disinfecting the life beneath, and the coldness
Afterwards felt by the absence of the tiny
Creatures that called this patch of life home.
Only to breed a new life of dogged progress
And change that the desert wind and sand Battle with to cover up mean While we build a new city
in the desert
And with it bring new pollution, pain and joy.

My God! Where am I?
Where should I go?
The cruel cities will eat at my soul,
But without these conveniences   The wraith
and shadow both will starve. My soul is strong
But still my soul bleeds.
The sirens and waves of men
Frightened by the beauty
Thus, luring her into sweet silence This is the only way they know, how to continue on.
Continue on, my son.

I'm chilled by the shadows that I stand in, But
still do not think I can run On my own without
her in the sun.
Each day she grows weaker as the
Polluted sky grows bleaker
Evermore the sky grows farther away,
My dreams upon the clouds that
Deliver acid into it all.

The Dark Woods

Despite the beautiful scenery and the quiet atmosphere, Devon and Estrella fought loudly and vocally in their vehicle. The tall and ancient forest was enchanting despite the pounding rains that beat in monsoon force upon the giant redwood trees and the small Volkswagen van. The chilling rains pounded upon their car like a persistent migraine and it seeped through the leaks in their rickety van to dampen their already sour temperaments. Devon drove much too fast for the winding highway 101 and could not be persuaded to slow down to look at the beautiful scenery of the Redwood forests of Humboldt County. He loathed the visit to Estrella's sister in Berkley California who had summoned them to assist her recovery from yet another nervous breakdown.

Even though the locals in Arcadia California warned against the winding roads and the pounding rains, Estrella thought it would be fun to 'take the adventurous route' down the twisted coastal highway 101. The rain didn't scare them and it was the first time either of them had been through these enchanting forests and Estrella laughed with childish glee each time they stopped and ran through the warm thick rains. Devon was not so enthusiastic as he drove white knuckled down steep switchbacks and up the narrow winding two lane highway, surrounded only by imposing redwood giants they got an occasional glimpse of the ocean as they crested the lightly traveled hills.

It was near sunset when Estrella asked Devon to pull over so she could relieve herself in the bushes. Devon found a narrow dirt pullout to ease into and Estrella jumped out of the van laughing and screaming in delight as she hugged an enormous redwood then squatted in the ferns at its base.

"I wonder what kinds of fairies live in these forests!?" Estrella said as Devon ran around the back of the van to urinate beside her.

"I don't believe in such rubbish!" Devon spat.

"Oh, don't be such a prude you jerk!" Estrella said. "Look at those beautiful mushrooms and tell me that some Fairies don't live here." Estrella ran into the forest and Devon reluctantly followed.

"Of Faries! Come out come out wherever you are!"

"There's probably only mean forest guardians like the sasquatch who attack anyone threatening their trees!" Devon growled as he chased Estrella down in his strong grip and playfully bit into her neck.

"Oh, you beast!" Estrella squealed in protest. She backed into a tree and let Devon sniff at her hungrily like a beast-man. As she looked over his shoulder, she saw movement back in the thick of the woods and glittering eyes flash briefly through fallen branches.

"I need a break from driving, what do you say we have a quickie out here?" Devon said as he rubbed his hand up his lover's thigh.

Estrella pushed him away and took a few steps into the woods, searching for another glimpse of the strange creature. "I don't know. I think there's something out there. I felt it watching us." "What?" Devon exclaimed.

"I don't know maybe it was my imagination but I want to leave." Estrella said with a suddenly bad feeling in her gut.

"Ok, get in the van." Devon said dejectedly.

Estrella had just barley shut her door when Devon stepped on the gas. The van shuttered and shook as the back tires spun uselessly in the mud. "Shit!" Devon exclaimed and hit the steering wheel. They got out to look at the tires, the back ones were sunken into the saturated soil. Devon cursed again and kicked the back bumper, then he screamed and gave the van a big push. To their surprise, it rolled forward on its own about ten feet into the forest before crashing into a tree. Devon screamed and Estrella laughed. This irked him even more and he climbed in the front seat to back out, yet again the tires dug into the mud.

"Well I guess we aren't supposed to leave!" He yelled in frustration as he climbed out of the van. Just then a truck came roaring into view, its headlights nearly blinding in the darkening dusk. Devon waved his arms and shouted to get the driver to stop but the truck barley slowed and even managed to kick up some muddy water at Devon as it drove by. More laughter at his back made him turn in anger, only it was not the familiar light laughter of his lover and as he looked around for her, she was not to be found.

"Estrella!" He called.

In response, strange giggles mixed with the pattering raindrops.

"Estrella! Come out! This isn't funny!" He cried, yet the rain and trees swallowed his voice. He walked unsteadily into the darkening forest calling out for his love when suddenly the sick laughter splashed over Estrella's voice.

"Devon, help me!" Came her panic-stricken wail.

Devon ran into the woods in the direction of the voice, and all around him he heard strange noises. The trickling water is just the background for a chorus of mocking insects that chirp and laugh, and high above are cawing ravens bidding good night to the cloud choked sun. Yet once more he hears Estrella's panicked plea only feet away.

He stumbled over a large fallen trunk as he came around a group of ancient trees. Thoughts of nightmare dreams battle with the reality of what he sees before him. Estrella is lying on the ground surrounded by half a dozen elfish demons that tear at her clothes and flesh with hungry glee. Estrella is helpless in their combined attack; their clawed hands hold her down as their dark furry heads delve into her skin with sharp teeth. Devon cries out in panic and the little demons glare at him before they take hold of Estrella by her hair and ribbons of flesh.

Just as he runs to her, the demons pull her into the hollow of a tree and disappear. Estrella's muffled screams echo through the trunk and he tries to dive in after her but can only grasp Estrella's booted foot. He pulls, and with a sickening noise the boot comes free into his hands, the severed foot still attached. Devon screamed again and tore at the hollowed entrance only to be slashed by sharp claws. One more try gives way only to rotting bark, nothingness, and pattering silence.

In despair and madness, he falls to the ground clutching Estrella's foot to his chest as he cries her name into the blasted forest. "Estrella!!!"

As he beats at the trees around him, he is suddenly aware of little beady eyes gathering around him. Determined not to follow the fate of his lover, Devon gets up and begins to run blindly into the forest while small demons no taller than his knees nip at his heels. They laugh and bite at his calves until he is running in pain and blindness. The edge of the cliff catches him by surprise as suddenly he is falling through rocks and roots down a steep incline to the beach below.

Black surf licks coldly at his toes and from above, the grimacing demons slowly climb down the steep ascent. Devon finds he has two choices; to swim or die. Regretfully he lies Estrella's booted foot down on the beach and takes his outer clothes off. He looks back to see the demons clinging to the tree roots watching him with hungry eyes.

With a deep sigh and a quick prayer to a God he has no name for, he plunged into the cool water and began to swim into the ocean as far as he could go.

Dark Woods Song

Very scary very scary.
Deep dark woods are very scary. Whooo!

Chorus
It isn't very good
In the dark, dark wood
In the middle of the night
When there isn't any light

What could be out there
Open your eyes and stare
In the cold black air
Are there monsters anywhere?

Chorus

What was that sound
There are voices all around
Are there demons in the night Who would like us for a bite?

Chorus

The Fairies that I see
They are hidden in the trees
But I see their lights, And its such a welcome sight!

Gods We Are

I was sitting in a small coffee shop talking with Gabe. A man I had known for years. I thought I knew everything about this man; I'd worked with him for years and had formed a solid friendship with him. We often went to each other's houses for dinner and desert and what not. I never thought much about the locked door at the end of the hall. I asked him what it was once and he came up with something about it being a storage area. But you never can guess what can be hiding behind closed doors.

We had just sat down and were sipping our coffee. Neither of us had anything much to talk about so we sat in silence until the waitress came with our salads. "I'm sorry, "I said to the waitress. "But I wanted blue cheese dressing, not thousand island." "Oh God" She said humbly, "Let me go fix that for you." She took my plate and disappeared into the back kitchen.
Gabe only laughed at me. "You're so picky!" He said.
"Well, I don't like thousand island OK?"
"That waitress is cute."
"Oh, God Gabe that's all you think about, isn't it?"
"Why did you say that?"
"Because it's true!"
"No I mean, why did you say oh God? I've never heard you swear before."
"I don't know, maybe because the waitress said it." I look at the salad that Gabe had started eating and asked. "Do you believe there is a God?" My brother had just died recently, and I had been having a hard time dealing with his death.
Gabe, short for Gabriel, suddenly changed his casual demeanor. He dropped the fork he had been pushing the salad around with and looked at me with a piece of lettuce hanging out of his mouth. If he wasn't all the sudden so serious, it would have

been funny. "That's an odd question." He said not giving me an answer.

"What's so odd about theology?"

"Oh nothing!" He pushed his plate away as if he had lost his appetite.

"Well?"

"Well what?"

"Do you believe in God?"

"I think it's time I showed you something I've done." He said. "Come over to my house tomorrow around noon."

"Are you going to fix me lunch?"

"Sure, just come over."

"So, what are you going to show me?"

"Just something I've been working on for a while." He picked up his fork again as the waitress returned with my salad. "So, did you go to the opera last night?"

"As a matter of fact, I did."

"Well then you must tell me all about it."

I knew he had purposely changed the subject, but that was the way my friend was and I knew it was hopeless to try to get him to talk about anything he didn't want to.

As scheduled, I arrived the next day at noon. Gabe answered the door frantically and quickly ushered me into the small kitchen. He looked very haggard as if he had just gotten out of bed and hadn't even bothered to brush his teeth. He was wearing a white lab coat over some pajamas and house slippers on his feet.

Hastily, he put together peanut butter and jelly sandwiches and two cans of soda pop. "I know this isn't a very good lunch," he said. "But I what I'm about to show you will make it up to you." He looked me over quickly and asked if I would take off my watch. I put it on the counter, and took a sandwich and followed him down the hall to the door that had always been locked ever since I had known him.

He pulled out a key and started to unlock the door, then thought better. "Before I show you this," he said as he turned around to face me. "I want you to promise me that you will never in your whole life tell a single soul about what I am about to show you."

"What are you going to show me?"

"I can't tell you unless you promise."

"Ok, I promise. What is it?"

"I'm serious. Not a single soul."

"Ok, I won't tell anyone."

"Promise?"

"Yes, yes, I promise."

"I can't believe I'm finally doing this." He said, "Here you must put this on over your clothes." I donned a white lab coat that matched his as he unlocked the door and held it open for me. He seemed very nervous and anxious and hesitated a few more times before he led me down a narrow flight of stairs that led into his basement.

It had never been finished, and the basement was the size of his house with no walls. The small windows along the top of the walls didn't let out very much light, which is why he had set up huge lamps at regular intervals around the area. The room was crowded with several tables pushed together to make one. On top of them was a model town, the kind people put together for a hobby. I however, had never seen a model town that was this detailed and large. At first glance I could make out the Town Square, the suburbs, even the dump. "This is cool." I said. "But why can't I ever tell anyone about it?"

The streets looked like a model of a small town only the colors were quite off. The hills and trees grew red and purple, a dark blue lake was rimmed by an orange beach and the buildings took on the many hues of the rainbow. The ceiling of the room was bright orange like an evasive omnipotent sun.

He leaned over the glass barrier that surrounded it and said. "Look closer."

The first thing I saw moving was a carriage pulled by two miniature horses in the nearest suburb. "What the...?"

"Amazing, isn't it?" I looked up and down the street and noticed the hundreds of insect sized people moving about and going about the business of everyday life except without the convenience of modern technology.

"What are they?"

"Well they are people that I created from myself. I am their God."

"You mean you created these people?"

"From my own image. Yes."

"But how?"

"Well it started out as a hobby." Gabe said. "You know the town and the buildings. It started out simple, but soon I became obsessed with detail. I wasn't content to just buy a plastic model house, I hand built them all. I would spend days, weeks, even months at a time in this room sometimes not even getting anything done, just staring at my town, and picturing all the people who lived here. Then one day I think I bumped my head and fell asleep on the table. I dreamed for days of the people in my town. Right down to their names and occupations. They couldn't have ears; or else the sound of my voice would surely deafen them, so they all speak in sign language and the written word. I dreamed of every detail. The pets they owned, their hobbies, everything. When I awoke, I first felt something on my hand. I opened my eyes without moving, and there were three insect sized men crawling around my hand trying to move it off a house. It startled me so much, that I jumped up and killed the men. I looked about and there they were. Hundreds of them. I know I dreamed them up, but they all seemed to act like they had lived their whole lives and didn't just pop up. I couldn't believe my eyes.

"I watched them for months, years in their time. They are so much smaller than we are that they move faster and die faster. I watched as generations were born. I watched them perform funerals and weddings, and celebrations of all kinds. Then I started to interact with them in small ways. They can't see beyond about two feet so it is safe for us to sit here and watch them. But I started giving them things they needed, like food and water. I taught them to gather their waste and to pile it here." He pointed to the dump. "And every now and then I would gather it up and dispose of it.

"I taught them to worship me. I wrote up in their language rules and laws they must obey. They must worship me in the open fields in groups and I will grant their wishes if I see it fit. If they all want something badly, they must write it down in a large script so I can retrieve it and read it. The things they ask for are food, water, longer life, care for the stricken and cures for injuries. Some of the things I can give them. Others they do for themselves and give the credit to me."

"You mean, you really are a God?"

"Yes!" He clutched my hand so tightly that it hurt. "And I want you to be a God with me."

"You want to make me a God of these people?"

"Yes."

"Why? I don't understand."

"The reason I took you here today is because I need to pass it on to someone I can trust to take care of my beloved children. I went in for my medical checkup a few months ago, and they found cancer in my body. They say I only have another month to live."

"Gabe...Oh God!"

"You called?" He said with a sheepish grin on his face. "I want to make you a god. Please say you will."

"I... I... I don't know if I can. What would I have to do?"

"Well, as I told you, you just have to do your best to fulfill their wishes, you know, feed them clean up a little, love them." He looked in my eyes and I saw that tears were forming in his. "I will give you the house. I can give my estates to anyone I want since I don't have any living relatives. I want to give it to you. I love you and I think you could do it."

"I have to think about it. It's not just something that one can just do. I have other obligations in my life Gabe. I just don't know if it's possible."

"I can introduce you to them. You can't pronounce their names, because they only speak in sign language. It's American Sign; it's what I know and they were created from my dreams so they can only do what I know. That's why I need you too. I need you to dream them new things and lives. You can reinvent this town after it's yours if you wish. All you have to do is dream of it in here and it can and will happen.

"Look, this woman with all the children. She is (--==)" He pointed to a small woman surrounded with several children and made a sign to say her name, "she runs the day care for the people in this suburb while the rest of them work. Here, the man on the carriage, he is (==-*) a deliveryman. He works with their version of the post office. And here is (++*-) working to grow a miniature crop of vegetable in his field."

"Gabriel," I interrupted as I took his hands in mine. "I don't know what to say."

"Say that you will take care of them." His eyes looked very hollow as he pleaded with me, and now that I looked, I could see the stress of the cancer weighing on his body and soul.

"I'll think about it, Ok?"

"Ok." He said. "Do you know sign language?"

"Yes, a little."

"Then take this one." He leaned over the glass and plucked up a man walking by himself in an empty field. "This is (++**)" he signed with his left hand while he held the befumbled man in his right. "Take him with you; I will even give you something to hold him in while you go home. I already printed up a note on my computer that is small enough for him to read, explaining that you are his God and he is to tell you of all the happenings in the town." "Gabe, your serious aren't you."

"Yes. I want you to become their new God." He placed the little man in my palm and he sat down in the curve of my fingers. "Come on, I'll show you out. Be careful with him." "I

will." I promised.

We finished the lunch of sandwiches. Gabe ate two and I picked at mine. I had lost any appetite I had had earlier and only wanted to go wake up in my bed and realize that this was all a strange dream. "There's just one more thing I have to tell you." He said.

"What's that?"

"I have been very careful to not give them technology, and I hope you think a very seriously before you give it to them. After all, look at what it did to our culture! I am convinced that technology will be the end of humanity and the longer our people go without it, the better chance they will have to survive a peaceful life. That's why I wanted you to leave your watch up here. I don't want them to come in contact with it. Here it is by the way." He handed me my watch, which I had forgotten about. "Please think about it very seriously." He pleaded. "I'm dying, and I can't leave them to die too. I've already seen an increase in disease with them and I know it's because of me. They need a healthy God, and one who will love them." He ushered me out the door with another plead to care for the little man I had, and to please say yes to his offer.

I went home and talked with (++**) who frantically told me of the troubles the village was having. He said that his people were dying from some unknown cause, Gabe had told them that I was going to save them and that I had to be their caretaker and dream for them now that Gabe was sick. He explained how Gabe dreamed their lives for them and since he was dying, so were they. They needed a new God and that was to be me.

I talked with little (++**) for hours. He sat on a book on my kitchen table and leaned back to take in my huge frame. He said that he was the only one who had met Gabe and acted as the priest for the rest of the village. Gabe told him to meditate when he was not in direct contact with him and every word Gabe said was followed to the tee.

Finally, I grew weary with exhaustion and gave the little man a place to sleep in some cloth scarves. Even though I was exhausted, I tossed and turned all night. I dreamt of little people crawling all over me and begging me to make them well. I woke in a cold sweat and hopped out of bed to brush of the wraiths I had imagined. I tried for another half-hour to sleep, but when I couldn't I took a long bath and tried to read a novel.

When I got up to eat breakfast and tend to my tiny charge, I found folded in the scarves the husk of the little man I had brought home with me. He was dead and I debated all morning as to what I should do with his body. My first reaction was to throw him away or flush him down the toilet like a dead fish. Finally, I decided to bury him in a shoebox in the back yard like one would do with a cat or mouse.

I had just returned to the kitchen to wash my hands when the phone rang. I was expecting it to be Gabe wanting an answer from me. Instead it was a policeman to inform me that Gabe had died that morning. He informed me that he had been found in his front yard by a jogger. In his front pocket of his shirt were his identification and a copy of his will, giving his house and all possessions to me along with explicit instructions that no one was to enter his house except me. The police officer asked me to come down to the hospital to identify the body and to sign some paper work.

I grudgingly went to the hospital, and left four hours later after being interrogated as to my relation to the man and my whereabouts the morning before. Apparently, Gabe had overdosed on a heart stimulate and died essentially of a heart attack. I was asked all the usual questions and told that the police would be getting back with me. I was given a key to Gabe's house and left.

I drove around for a few hours taking in the sights of the city. The tall buildings and heavy traffic and of course the smog and pollution and crime that went along with it. I went to my office building and recalled how Gabe had left a few months ago on a sick leave and never returned. I gathered up the pile of letters and memos in my inbox and left. I drove around procrastinating the inevitable. Finally, when the sun began to lower in the sky I went to Gabe's house and let myself in.

The End; or maybe the beginning…

This is a Living Soul

What if all these snowflakes were souls?
Billions of the living for a few seconds to a few months Some of them gaining relative fame as they are glimpsed by some mortal being or melting on a nose or tongue.
Some of the forming a pack such as a snowball or snowman.
Yet for every one of these flakes there are
Thousands still that slowly dissolve away into
Silence and obscurity.

How I Got My Dreadlocks
(3-23-03)

Illustration Photo by Gothic Michael

The year was 1999 and I had decided that spring to drop out of college and teach myself the skills I would need for the rest of my life. I was dreadfully tired of my hometown of Salt Lake City and GreenWVich was to be my escape ticket; a two-toned puke/lime green 1977 Volkswagen Vannagon Camper Van. It was mid Augusts and I had just made this marvelous purchase from a woman who swore that werewolves and the government were after her so she couldn't drive out there anymore or they would find her. I had just eaten an enormous dinner at my hang out Le China Bleu, the house of local street artists to whom I owe my roots in performing.

I didn't want to, couldn't go home to my parent's house so I set off for a spur of the moment camping trip in my new ride. No one was particularly game to go except of course my dog Arkaia a black and white furry border collie- lab mix. Her name Arkaia means Ancient Fairy or as I refer to her, My Shadow. Her most two favorite places to go in the world are the forests and the cemeteries and she's color coordinated to me with white paws and chest like my bare feet and stomach, the rest uniformly dressed in black.

I borrowed some blankets and food for breakfast to cook on the Vannagon's built in stove. With fresh songs in my heart I headed up the back trails of the Wasatch Mountains that surround Salt Lake. I cranked up a tape of KMFDM or perhaps it was White Zombie and searched out a road I'd never seen before.

Although I had lived there my whole life, it didn't take me long to get gloriously lost on a thin winding dirt road that twisted up the side of the mountain. As I often tell my friends "I have a great sense of direction and an equally strong sense of adventure!
So, don't be surprised if I get lost for the hell of it!"

As the trees grew tall around us, and we climbed in elevation, Arkaia whined softly in anxious anticipation of running through the woods and chasing squirrels and birds. I wasn't quite sure what I was looking for, but my directional instincts told me to keep driving past the logged clearings and even through a shallow creek that ran over the dirt track.

Abruptly the road ended as the sun began its colorful descent in the sky, lighting up the clouds in a brilliant display of red and oranges and yellow-gold lining around the sun. The wind blew in cool moist gusts that dredged up the smell of the lake and thick bubbly clouds. Before me I saw a small cabin, an old shack and fire pit outside. The forest around us was a mix of scrub oak, pine and scattered stands of aspen.

I shut off the bus and opened the door. The pleasant smell of fresh woods and sweet wild flowers washed over me as Arkaia jumped over my lap and ran around in quick excited circles. I walked up to the small abandoned hut. The walls were made of natural wood logs from the surrounding forests. The locks on the wood door had been previously pried off and the door hung ajar swaying invitingly in the low wind. In front of the hut was a stone fire pit and a beautiful nearly perfect fairy ring of mushrooms, decorated with delicate little purple and red flowers.

As I knelt to examine the ring, I swear I heard giggling behind and above me as if from the trees. I looked over my shoulder and my dog was hopping through the sparse underbrush chasing something to the base of a tree and sniffing through the roots. I turned again to examine the ring of mushrooms in front of me. They were brown and gray with red and white spots, thick stalks and caps the size of my palm. The flowers grew in little clusters of 3's and 5's around the rind broadening its boarders to stretch into the small open clearing.

It looked all too inviting and I couldn't resist the temptation to jump the boarder of the ring and sit in the center of this magical apex. "Flee to me remote elf!" I cried in jest and laughed at my wise crack for pulling off a good palindrome. I said it two more times then, after I got over my giggles I calmed down enough to close my eyes and contemplate the wisdom (if any) of that moment. A faded image came to my mind of fairies dancing in a ring around the mushrooms. They glowed with their own white light that illuminated the mushrooms at their feet, upon which they danced around. Quickly the image faded again.

The sun was out of sight from the trees and was probably just meeting the far horizons. The sky above me was already dark and the horizon glowed pinkish-red. I only had a few minutes of light left so I sprang to my feet and jumped out of the circle again. The wind blew through my shoulder-length straight blonde hair and long skirts as I danced in my own circles around the ring of mushrooms. In three circles, I ran while singing and dancing in twisting spirals of erratic movement that suddenly came upon me.

The sky grew darker and darker with each passing second so I skipped to my van and pulled out my small pocket-sized flashlight and my handmade black and magenta cloak.

I pulled open the door to the shack that was skewed open and after flashing my light around briefly I entered.

The wooden floor creaked under my feet and I could see where it was rotted through to some places and the dirt was visible below. There were three rooms in the small cabin; the front room had some sparse decaying furniture in it, (an old couch and a couple of broken chairs). The walls were covered in faded paintings of trees, fairies, forest animals and mushrooms. The art was done in a simple style of big brush strokes and undefined figures. Still I could pick out the shapes of crows and eagles, deer and lizards.

In the next room, there were some old kitchen components and crumbling counter tops. A pile of rags decomposed in the corner and three or four small children's shoes littered the floor. The third room was the size of a walk-in closet and it was empty save for a pile of children's shoes scattered all over the floor. They were all different styles and sizes from little infant shoes to medium children's shoes and only a few larger adult-size women's shoes.

I thought it odd, took note of it, and walked over to examine them closer. I picked up a shoe only to find it occupied by a rat! I dropped it back in the pile in surprise and a few more rats scurried away giving me a good look at their pretty and unusual black and white stripes.

Again, I heard a chittering outside as if from a small creature laughing. I looked around and saw that my dog had chased something outside, she was whining strangely and I felt a stab of fear run through me as I rushed outside.

At first sight the clearing offered nothing unusual. Arkaia was standing in the clearing outside and looked at me with relief as I came out to her. She ran to me wagging her whole body as well as her tail. I kissed her face then ran to the end of the clearing feeling exuberant and free, she was right behind me ready to go as I was.

With a cry of excitement, we took off for our adventure and I even let Arkaia lead us into the forest, and she scampered on ahead as if she was onto the trail of something. With my flashlight on I wandered through the darkness behind 'my shadow' the darkest thing out there prancing about, as we walked I softly sang our night time adventure song.

>Me and my shadow,
>Walking down the street.
>Me and my shadow,
>Wondering who we'll me.
>Me and my shadow,
>What will we see today?
>
>See the little fairies hiding in the bushes.
>See the pixies laughing way up in the trees.
>Are they casting spells now, are they flying by
>Are they making dreams for the stars up in the sky?
>All the little fairies, watch how they fly on by.
>
>Ba da da da dat dat bum da da dat.
>Ba da da da dat bam da dat.
>
>Walkin through the city, see whats on the street.
>There be strange people out there that we'll meet.
>Jump at them my shadow, chase them far away.
>All that matters now is you and me today.
>Me and my shadow, what will we see today?
>
>Ba da da da dat dat bum da da dat.

Ba da da da dat bam da dat.

We found a small creek whose waters were surprisingly warm. I took off my shoes to wade through the water. The bottom was smooth and the water came to my knees and I had to lift my skirt up to my waist so it wouldn't get wet. I found it so inviting that I couldn't resist the temptation to take off the rest of my clothes and throw them to the side of the creek. With a big breath, I dunked my whole body into the chill water. I stood with a scream and shook out my shoulder-length straight hair. The icy mud beneath my fingers and toes tried to steal my breath away and I arose from its shivery grasp I gasped for sweet air. My nerves were screaming with sensation! A cool breeze ran around me and whispered in the trees, carrying my scent away like the water under my feet. Unseen frogs and crickets chirruped around me and, was that laughter I heard again? I couldn't be sure.

I dunked my body in the creek again and squealed the water was so cold! It made my body tingle with electricity that makes me feel so alive! Chittering mountain winds rushed down to the valley as the slivered Cheshire Moon peeked down through the trees and clouds. I scrambled into my clothes and huddled in my cloak for a few moments, my body shivering from the sudden chill.

Arkaia had been waiting for me to soak, but when I stood she jumped around in anxious leaps, ready to keep going, to continue our adventure. I turned on the flashlight and found another thin path that looked like it ran up the side of the mountain. Eagerly we blazed through the hills, a few times I got my hair snagged in hanging tree branches as we climbed the mountainside the trees became smaller and the path scarcer.

Not knowing where we were going, I soon ran into a thicket of bushes that prevented any further advance up the valley. I climbed and pushed my dog up the tall rocks that rose above the bottom, finally we came to a level ledge that looked over the forested valley. The city was out of sight, yet the sky held an eerie glow from the lights reflecting on the clouds above. The wind pushed thick dark clouds across the sky. I sat down next to my dog and watched the clouds take strange shapes; dark cats and flying dragons eating up the stars that twinkled faintly.

I tried to light a stick of sage but any whips of smoke I managed to coax out of it with my lighter were taken with the wind. I laughed as the moon smiled and winked at me then quickly faded from sight like an elusive cat. "Cheshire Moon, I see you!" I called to it and again it revealed only half its wry grin to me. I pulled out a large quartz crystal and pointed it to the moon. "I call upon you Sister Luna! Come out here and speak to me a moment." I said.

I sat up straight and folded my legs beneath me. I shared the warmth of my cloak with my familiar and called upon the Goddess Gaia of the Earth, the Singing Voices of the Wind, to Kali, to Destructa of Fire, and to Death the West and Water. I asked for certain secrets to be revealed to me and for my destiny to seek me out. Droplets of water fell upon me as I called to the shadows and Fairies to grace me with their magical presence.

A gust of wind blew my hood off my head and rushed through my ears. The rain drummed softly to the ground. I laughed at the clouds that lightly showered down and called to them. "Wash away my impurities so I may fly as a different creature."

I sat there for a few more minutes until I realized that the rain wasn't going to let up. I slowly rose to my feet with numb legs and stinging feet. I put my hood back on and looked around for my flashlight. It was nowhere to be found, I crawled around on the ground for a few minutes looking for it. Perhaps the Pixies had taken it for their own little toy. I don't know but I couldn't find it. I started to panic a little, unsure of what to do or where to go to get back. Way down there I thought I saw a darker patch of black in the forest that could have been where the clearing and little house were. I had to get out of the rain so carefully and nearly blind I headed down the mountain through the trees. The trail that had taken me up here was below the steep rocks so I guessed a new direction I needed to head in and trailblazed through the brush with my dog Arkaia right at my heels.

I walked around the biggest bushes while I pushed my way through the smaller ones. The pine trees got thicker and every few steps another one grew, most of them with branches tall enough that I could walk under them. I stopped a few times to hug the large tress around me and listen to their calm voices. I asked them which direction I could go to get out but they wouldn't tell even if they knew.

I stumbled through the woods, tripping over vines and roots, the rain coming down harder to beat at the leaves and ground. Thunder flashed and lit up the thick forest. The noise around me was getting louder, the chirrups and chittering of the insects growing into an orchestra of foreign noise. I became fearful with the suspicion that someone or something was watching me. I looked over my shoulder, scanning the darkness and fell, scratching my ankle on a thick root.

I felt blood running down my leg and I sat to examine it. The damage wasn't too bad so I smeared away the blood and wiped my hand on the nearest tree. When I stood again, I saw little flickering lights in the thick woods ahead and heard faint laughter echo in the bushes all around.

"Hello!" I said. "Who's there?"

The only answer I heard was once again their laughter. I cried out to them again, "Hello? What are you? I am Autumn of these mountains. I order you to show yourselves!"

A flash of lightening lit the area for a second and was quickly followed by booming thunder. I cringed and held onto my trembling dog at my side. I heard a twig snap behind me. As I turned to look, a flash of lightening showed me a stark form crouching around a tree. I gasped as its growl turned into the booming thunder all around me. Like a dark vision from a spectral nightmare, the shadowy creature raced upon me with his claws ready to pounce and tear. He had a handsome face with a dark beard and goatee, his yellow glowing cat eyes gleamed under large curling horns. He wore fur stoles on his shoulders and hips. I did not notice at first but he had strong hooves in place of feet.

I turned to run and heard twigs snapping apart just behind me. I glanced over my shoulder then crashed into a tree behind me with such force that I was knocked down to the ground. I scrambled to turn over just in time to see him pounce upon me with flashing eyes big as shooting stars.

"Fly with me!" He hissed and breathed into my mouth. His breath was cloying and strange in my lungs. It was intoxicating and sent me to a strange place.

My spirit rose out of my body with a shocking rush, sending me to join in the spiraling energy of the great goddess. She caught me in a large spiraling web that spun through the universe. I was consumed by her massive power that ate all in its path and burned it as fuel that fired new creation. I felt as if I was carried through the wheel of fortune to the place I needed to go in order to gain the practical knowledge necessary for my destiny. I saw a wide river with paddleboats and sweet jazz music pouring from the paving stones around me. Fog closed in but I felt her name, "New Orleans!"

The Satair (or Panageriee (creature of Pan) as I came to think of him) clawed at my blonde hair and whispered strange worlds. Soft fur and a thick musky smell surrounded me in the thick forest rain. I grasped for the trees around me and managed to regain to my feet while long fingers and branches pulled at my cloak and skirts. Arkaia jumped at the Satair between us and distracted the Satair while I started down the hill again. Thick brush hindered my progress and in my panic I fell into a sunken hole.

Then I was taken to a void, falling into violet darkness I reached out and screamed. A beautiful Fairy Queen with iridescent wings and a light flowing body flew to me and by taking my hand, led me to her haven where the Fairies held court. The tiny light creatures surrounded me with laughter and light touches. Were those the flashing lights and laughter I'd spied earlier? Like a hoard of hungry insects, they surrounded me as if I were covered with honey. Their little bodies were between two and five inches of iridescent swirling light that moved so quickly it was hard to distinguish their bodies' actual shape. The dark forest shrieked with shrill cries and laughter as forest spirits taunted me into their dance.

Chatting and buzzing among themselves as they plucked at my hair, skin, and clothes. I tried to fight the Fairies off at first, but stopped when I heard the meaning of the song they sang to me.

Come down here to where the Fairies play,
Dance with us for a night and a day
We shall teach you the secrets of the Fey,
Lay your clothes off like a fluttering moth
Our magic makes new cloth
That's finer that yours and very soft.
Dance with us now in our Fairy ring
Show us what gifts you did bring
And laugh with us as we all sing
Trust to your feet and to your heart To
let the magic do its part
Follow our rites with our ancient art.
Come down here to where the Fairies play
Dance with us forever and a day S,o we
may teach the secrets of the Fey.

Faster and faster they danced around me, the Panigeree demon twirled me by the arm until I finally fell to the earth in dizzy exhaustion they again fell upon me. They danced around and around with leering faces, whimsically human yet with insectial expressions. Their small bodies glowed faintly of their own light that flickered magically.

I tried to brush them off when the Fairies tangled in my hair, but there were many and they were persistent. The panigeree danced and capered before me, making me laugh as the Fairies flew round him. They chattered and chirruped in a feral tongue I could not understand. Then the Panigeree turned to me and bowed. "Welcome to our garden" He said before his beautiful form flickered and faded from sight. The Fairies sang a discordian harmony to me and suddenly exhaustion took hold of me so that I could only moan in my delirious state of enchanted sleep. I felt them crawling through my hair and over my skin like electrical insects. Their tingling touches sent exotic shivers through my body.

This onslaught of Fairy feelings eventually overcame my senses and I retreated to the respite of sleep.

How long had I lain there I could not tell but I woke up shivering from the cold as morning dew gathered on my nearly naked body. In the pale light the last of the Fairies scattered to hide as I looked around me. All I wore was one of my two skirts and one sock. My body was sore as if I'd stretched and stressed every muscle in my body, and I had little scratches all over my skin.

Weakly, I rose on shaking limbs and crawled out of the shallow hole I had fallen into. Colorful mushrooms sprouted from the decaying logs all around me in another fairy ring. Thick brush surrounded this little hole and tall trees filtered out the sunlight. I looked around for my clothes in the dewy half-light, and found my shirt nearby and my other skirt hanging from some brushes.

While I put these on I called for my dog Arkaia. She was nowhere in sight and the more I called for her the worse I felt. Quickly I scoured the ground for my missing sock and shoes, but they were nowhere to be found! While searching however, I noticed I was in the middle of a patch of four leaf clovers! Next to that, some strange and beautiful mushrooms grew out of a fallen tree. I picked a few of the clovers before continuing my search for my dog and my cloak.

I found my cloak back in the trees a little way off. It was on the ground in a thick dark puddle. It looked like something dead was lying atop it, which scared me. Tentatively I touched the dark shape and felt my dog's soft hair. She startled, with a scared whine at my touch, then jumped into my arms and licked my face with soft whimpers. I picked up my cloak that she had been lying on and put it on despite the fact that it was wet and muddy.

My hair was disheveled and terribly matted so I put my hood on and walked down the hill behind my bouncing shadow who nervously led the way out. The sun was rising by the time I spied the stark green of my VW that contrasted with the green leaves around me.

I ran to it gratefully and found it just as I had left it. I climbed in and made up breakfast on the interior stove before driving out of there, making sure to leave some of my milk and pancakes behind for the Fairies in the center of their magical ring.

I tried at first to comb out my hair, but it was irrevocably knotted into long thin locks that had been tied together with many small hands. I let it go and finished the process with the rest of my hair to develop the lovely long blonde dreadlocks you see on me today.

So, that's how I got my dreadlocks. That's my story and I'm sticking to it!

Fairy Cocoon

In darkened shadows, they meet
Dancing on starlight on nimble feet.
In treetops. they swiftly fly
Where winded leaves sigh they gracefully lie After weeks of wooing and fine romance the two entwine for one last dance.

They start with a kiss that's tart and sweet
A hint of the bliss they find when they meet.
Garments are shed without a care and they embrace in the chill night air.
Soft skin shimmers in the faint light of the moon.
Soft skin shivers making Fairy lovers swoon.

Whispered words are echoes through the trees
And rumors fly between the birds and bees
Of a union of love that rings so true
And acts of lust that should be taboo.
Graceful long legs curl around arms
Colorful frail wings unfurl with round charms

Tangled legs and twisted toes
Cling to branches were flower buds grow
Like spider's silk a ring is spun
Its time now for this deed to be done
Two forces collide and fate is sealed
Cries of pain and pleasure ring through the field

Flesh enters flesh in a consuming mess
Weavers weave webbing in an ensnaring mesh
For countless hours and seconds, they lay
Together in bliss they wait for the day
They melt into a shapeless form

To felicitate some new life born.
Till on the most beautiful day in spring
When flowers bloom and all birds sing
From the silver cocoon, tiny fairies are cast
Into the new world alive at last
Thousands of tiny lights set free Lighting up the night for me!

The Bear and the Mountain

By Autumn Augustus

Once there was a great Brown Bear named MudWater. He was raised long ago in a cool valley of tall trees and big rocks. A big stream ran through the center of the valley for which he got his name for its banks were often sticky with thick mud. But the bears didn't mind the mud too much since they had plenty of room to romp around in and places to play. There were a few places in the stream where they could lay down their whole bodies in the summer time and bathe in the warm water. As the Bear MudWater grew into an adult, his parents taught him to hide from the humans who ran around always on two feet and wore strange furs.

One day, he watched his mother get shot with a fire stick and when she fell down the humans took her away. He ran to find the other bears to tell them what had happened and they told him to stay away from the humans.

"But why did they do that?" He asked in confusion.

"Go and see the elder bear FishFinder in his cave." The bears told him. "He can tell you some answers."

It was a good distance away and MudWater walked for two days to reach the elderbear FishFinder. His cave was small and musty and the old bear inside rested on a bed of weeds and mounded dirt. MudWater woke the old bear politely with soft nuzzles on his flank and the old bear looked up from his sleep with watery gray eyes. "Who is it that disturbs my sleep?" "It is MudWater, I have a question for you."

"What do you need I'm busy!" Growled the old bear.

"I want to know why the humans killed my mother."

"They killed her so they would have more room for themselves." Said FishFinder. Once we bears could roam anywhere, and we did without fear! But man came with his fences, houses and death so now we are confined to the mountains where they do not go so much.

"But why?"

"You have a hard question and in answer I will give you a quest!" Said the old bear. "Climb to the top of the mountain and perhaps there you will find the answers you seek and even see the Eyes of God."

"The Eyes of God?"

"That's what I said." Growled FishFinder.

"Why do I have to climb the mountain to find it?"

"I could try to tell you but you wouldn't understand until you saw it for yourself anyway." Said FishFinder. "You will climb the hills and follow the river to the top of the mountain. There you will understand."

"Does the river come from the top of the mountain?" "Too many questions! Go and seek the answers for yourself. You follow the river to the top of the mountain and you will see." At that FishFinder turned around in his bed and closed his eyes.

"I've never been that far, I'm afraid." Said MudWater.

In reply FishFinder started to snore.

Slightly disgruntled, MudWater walked away and headed for the river. It was cold and wide and only a few small fish swam in it during the summer. He ate berries instead of fish and started to walk up the river. Soon the way grew thick with trees and the big bear was forced to walk in the forest instead of the riverbank. He walked far up into the mountain and he soon began to wonder if there really was a top to it. After several days of walking, the bear stopped for a long rest in a small meadow.

His rest was disturbed by a fox who teased the bear and yapped at him. "This is my meadow, why are you sleeping in it?" Asked the fox.

"I am going to the top of the mountain to find some answers." Replied MudWater.

"How will the mountain show you the answers?" "The old bear FishFinder said I will see the Eyes of God there." "Ah, you seek enlightenment!" Said the fox.

"What is that?"

"It is a way to know everything and know God."

"Yes, I want to see the Eyes of God."

"You don't have to go to the top of the mountain to see the Eyes of God." Said the fox.

"I don't?"

"No, come let me show you something." The fox walked away and MudWater followed him. "I have received visions when I ate these." The fox stood in front of a small patch of colorful mushrooms.

"I don't know." Said the bear.

"You are a big bear, it won't hurt you try it."

MudWater ate the colorful mushrooms and the fox laughed and ran in circles. Shortly MudWater began to feel funny and uncomfortable. His vision began to play weird tricks on him and he stumbled around confused.

"How do you feel?" Asked the fox.

"Strange." Said the bear.

"Do you see God?"

The bear looked around him and up at the tall trees that swayed gently back and forth in the wind. They seemed to sing to each other in a way he had never noticed before. But when he thought of God his mind only grew heavy with thoughts that he didn't understand. "No, I just see the wind singing in the trees." Answered MudWater.

"Well, I thought it was a shortcut but maybe you do have to climb the mountain to find what you're looking for." Said the Fox and he ran away to chase a rabbit.

MudWater roamed around the clearing and looked at the plants growing out of the ground and only got confused when he tried to think of what God had to do with the trees and grass. He went back to sleep and dreamed of walking to the top of the cold mountain where even in the summer there was thick frosty snow. A voice spoke to him that said "Keep looking!" and he looked over the edge of the mountain and saw only clouds above and below him hugging the trees.

When he woke, he walked back to the river to drink some water and eat some roots and small fish. There were a few tree frogs sitting around and croaking to eachother and he tried to chase a few down. Finally, he caught one and it screamed for its life.

"Please don't kill me big bear!" Croaked the frog.

"But I am hungry." Growled the bear.

"I will teach you something if you don't eat me." Chirped the frog. "I am just a little tree frog named Leap and I want to live to raise my tadpoles."

"I am looking for the Eye of God." Said the bear. "If you can show me that I won't kill you."

"Yes, yes, I know a shortcut to God!" Said Leap. "Let me down and I will show you."

"If I let you down you will get away." Said the bear.

"Please, look into the stream out there where the water swirls around the rocks in a circle. There is a God in there I swear!"

"This better not be a trick!" Growled MudWater and he let the frog go so he could wade into the stream. The swirling water was cool and delicious and he looked down into it after taking a long drink and saw only the rocks in the bottom of the stream.

"Keep looking." Croaked Leap who jumped into the thick brush at the side of the stream.

MudWater looked deeper into the water and saw many small tadpoles swimming around. They were so small and fast that he couldn't catch any of them and he growled again and stomped up the stream in frustration. "There is nothing in there but tadpoles!" He roared.

"Yes, but they come from God!" Laughed the frogs on the side of the stream. MudWater didn't understand so he kept walking up the mountain.

A few days later big storm clouds gathered overhead and a cold wind foretold of heavy rain. A rich wet smell filled the air which MudWater could understand. He found some tall pine trees that gave good cover and he crawled underneath one as the rain started to pour down. There was a crow in the tree and it squawked at the bear.

"I am BlackWing the crow! What are you doing under my tree?"

"I am trying to stay dry." Said MudWater. "I am lost, can you tell me bird, am I going the right way to get to the top of the mountain?"

The crow laughed and hopped around on the ground outside the tree. "You want to find the top of the mountain? I can fly there but there are big rocks in the way that you won't be able to climb over."

"Maybe you can fly there and tell me what you see so I don't have to go there myself." Said the bear.

"Why do you have to go there?" Asked the crow.

"The old bear FishFinder told me that I would see the Eyes of God if I climbed the mountain." Said the bear. He was a little embarrassed now because he was beginning to doubt the purpose of his own quest.

"The Eye of God?" Squawked BlackWing. "I can tell you what you will see from the top of the mountain. You will see many trees and big people houses far far down in the valleys." "But where will I find God?" Asked the bear.

"Come out here in the rain." Said the bird.

The rain was coming down very heavily but the bear still followed the bird out into the pouring rain. "See how the dirt soaks in the water?" Asked the crow.

"Yes."

"It feeds it to the trees and the grass to make them grow. That is how God works, by making things grow and live see?"

"I'm just getting wet." Moaned the bear. "I get cold and I don't like it."

"The trees like it, they soak in the rain and then send it to all the leaves when the sun comes out again. It's the work of God."

"But what is the Eye of God?" Asked MudWater. "FishFinder told me that I would see the Eye of God when I climbed the mountain."

"There is a shortcut up the mountain if you walk up the creek." Said the Crow. "I don't know about the Eye of God but I know it will be quite a climb for you. Good luck!" BlackWing squawked and was answered by other crows in the trees above. He flew off and joined his friends while MudWater sat in the pouring rain and watched the trees and grass soak up the rain like his fur did.

"I still don't understand." Said MudWater and he pulled up some brush to chew on the moist roots. He took a few mouthfuls of roots under the tree and chewed on them till the rain let up.

When it stopped raining the next day, MudWater continued his journey up the mountain and BlackWing the crow was right, the way became very steep and hard to climb. He tried to follow the creek but it was slick and steep as well. On the side of the creek smaller bushes grew among the trees and he walked over these to find good footholds. He feasted on bugs under the rocks of the shallow stream bank while he rested during his climb. The higher he climbed, the more creeks he found that flowed into the stream he was climbing and he would sit in confusion wondering which one to follow. There were not many animals, way up there in the snowy heights of the mountain and all he could find to eat was bark and hard roots.

MudWater was almost ready to lose hope when he found a tall tower of rock that blocked his path up the mountain. There was a tall beautiful waterfall running down the rocks and some vines climbed up the rocks but they would not hold the big bear and he only fell down when he tried to climb the slick steep surface. He wailed in frustration and cursed at FishFinder who had put him on this silly quest in the first place.

A hawk heard him roaring and circled round him in the air before he landed nearby to talk to the bear. "What is the matter?" Asked the hawk.

"I'm trying to climb the mountain but I can't find a way past these tall rocks." Wailed the bear.

"You are a far way from home, I don't see any other bears up here trying to climb the mountain. What an ambitious bear you are!"

"I am trying to find the Eye of God." Said the bear.

"I understand." Said the hawk. "The view from the top of the mountain is certainly worth the effort to get up there. Maybe if you walk around this way you will find a way that is not so steep." The hawk flew around the mountain and the bear hurried to follow the quick bird.

"Here is a streambed that is not so deep." Said the hawk after MudWater had been following him for half a day. "Maybe you can climb up here."

"Have you seen the Eye of God?" Asked the bear as he started his climb.

"I have seen many things in my life, I can fly from the top of one mountain to another in the time it would take you to climb this little bit left. You are almost to the top don't stop now!" Encouraged MudWater continued to climb.

"What does it look like?" Asked the bear with anticipation.

"I can't tell you as well as your eyes can." Squealed the hawk.

Several times the bear slipped down the slick snow-covered rocks and earth as he climbed to the top of the mountain and the hawk circled round to point out better routes when the bear got stuck. "Why are you so helpful?" Asked the bear gratefully.

"Because I have never seen a bear climb the mountain before." Said the hawk. "Look here at this perch I sit on, you are almost there, hurry before the sun goes away."

The bear pushed himself up despite his tired bones and hungry stomach. He ate the snow in his path to quench the pit in his stomach but it only made him feel colder up there on the heights. A gentle wind blew under his thick fur and he huffed and puffed as he mounted the perch next to the hawk who hopped out of his way. MudWater felt so tired he wanted to collapse on the spot and wouldn't have looked up if the hawk hadn't told him to.

Suddenly he felt very dizzy as he looked down the steep mountain he had climbed. There were many trees below and broken clouds over the horizon that changed colors to the setting of the sun. "Oh!" Cried the bear. "It all looks so far away and small!"

"Yes." Said the hawk. "And do you see it? The Eye of God that you were looking for?"

The sun lowered over the horizon and turned the clouds all around into magnificent reds or oranges. "The setting sun?" Asked MudWater. "Is that it?" "You tell me." Said the hawk.

"Yes, I think it is."

"It gives life to all that you see below you." Said the hawk.

"Arr, I can see the sun from anywhere, I didn't have to climb up here to see it!" Growled MudWater.

"To see the whole picture, you did." Answered the hawk.

"But I still don't understand why the humans killed my mother."

"Do you see their big homes?" Asked the hawk.

MudWater looked below him and saw the big boxes that grew off the hills and filled the valleys far, far below. "Yes." Said the bear. "They look small from up here.

"They keep making more of them higher and higher up the mountains forcing all the animals up into the hills. They are like ants only bigger and they don't know where to stop."

"What about the Eye of God?"

"He sees it all and will reward each of his creatures as he sees fit." Said the hawk.

"Hum."

"So, was it worth it?"

"What?"

"To climb the mountain."

"Yes!" Declared MudWater. "I understand now! Those animals all tried to show me shortcuts to see god, the strange mushrooms, the tadpoles growing in the stream, the rain feeding the mountains. It's all connected, even with the humans and if I hadn't climbed all the way up here I wouldn't have understood."

"Very good." Said the hawk. "You are right, it is all connected."

"It's all natural and beautiful." Said MudWater wisely. "Their houses, the forests, the mountains, the sun! I see how the snow turns into the streams that feed us and how all of us animals have our perfect places here."

"What about the sun?" Screamed the hawk.

"It is very bright up here, but it shines on everything and sees all. Ahh the Eye of God!"

"Yes, and it loves all it touches. That is why it makes us warm."

MudWater thought on this a moment then asked, "Is that what enlightenment is?"

"You tell me." Said the hawk and he screamed into the air before he flew off and turned big circles overhead.

MudWater slept there for the night and watched the sun rise on the opposite side that it had set from. The hawk brought him a breakfast of half a rabbit to reward him for his effort to climb the mountain. "I think I have found it, now I must go back down to tell my friends of the Eye of God." Said MudWater. "Thank you for helping me."

"Your welcome, now you know that there are no shortcuts to hard work, and if you seek the deep answers of enlightenment the hard road is worth the rewards." "Yes, it is." Agreed MudWater.

"Tell your friends to come up here and I will help show them the way," said the hawk and then he soared off into the rising sun. MudWater watched the hawk fly away and when he passed in front of the sun the bird disappeared from sight.

Meet Me at the Spot

Meet again when you find this carving
Me in my dress blowing genlty in the wind
At the time we both felt love
The universe seemed to hide in your embrace   Spot
in my heart like a spot in the sun.

Illustration By Justin Caristo

The Show Must Go On
As told to me by Silvan the tightrope clown.

I was not very old when I first saw the circus. If it hadn't been for my unmindful father who left me to my own devices I might never had seen the circus like I had. At the time my father and I were living in a shack and he was working to get by with various day labor jobs. I guess I can say he tried to be a father to me sometimes but for the most part he was always absorbed in his drink and strange girls who would come over every now and then.

Not always knowing what to do with myself I often got into trouble around the poor neighborhood we lived in by stealing food and trespassing the neighbors yards and gardens. Still, I kept myself occupied enough to avoid the scorn of the general public or the police.

I was only nine years old the day the circus came to town. It was then the highlight of my meager life. The brightly painted trucks and vans and the strange people inside them. I was fascinated and I watched from afar as they set up the big circus tent as I was too shy to go over there. It took the greater part of a day to set up the tent and when they were done, hawkers ran through the streets selling tickets yelling all the while. "Circus Bizerkus! Circus Bizerkus! Come see the amazing circus!"

I searched frantically for my father to ask him for a ticket. I went to the bar, to his friend's house but could find him nowhere. As the show started, I gave up and sat outside listening to the cheers of the audience and the strange music that pounded forth from the massive tent. I cried in self-pity as I tried to imagine what could possibly be happening in there. Of course I knew that all I imagined would pale horribly in comparison to what those brightly painted clowns were up to. I sat there halfway through the show then ran home in hysterical tears.

Tom, my father, was unsympathetic to my pain but told me that I could go tomorrow if I found someone else to buy me a ticket. I went to sleep scheming up ways to afford the five-dollar cover...

In the morning I went back to the big circus tent and seeing no one around to patrol, I sneaked behind the tent walls. I remember the wonder I felt as I tried to take in the shear size of the temporary dome. I had known it was big from looking at it outside but I hadn't thought it was that big! Lines of bleachers surrounded a circular stage where some clowns were hanging out in disheveled costume. Not wanting to be seen, I hid behind some of the bleachers and watched them.

There were about a dozen clowns and they ran about each other with loud whooping noises and strange props like a giant hammer and nails. Then they would suddenly stop their running and talk about the next part. All the while passing around a short bottle of liquor and a fat cigar. I watched them quite amused for some time when a beautiful clown came walking out. She wore stripped stockings and ruffle pants and a big billowy shirt under a tight corset. Her makeup was of a sad clown and she wore a smart striped hat that matched her stockings. As she walked she jingled with the clacking of many bells and coins on her belt and wrists.

"OOOhhhh ahhhh Silver!" The clowns all ogled at her. "We like it. Are you going to be a clown now?"

She didn't say a word but basked about in their praise and nodded at being a clown. Then she picked up a diabolo and threw the spinning bob around and around on the thin string connected to the sticks in her hands. The clowns all cheered and praised her as she took a deep bow. She was just reaching for the offered cigar the clowns were passing around when the ringmaster came out with a booming voice.

"You can clown if you like Silver but you will still walk that tightrope!" His words struck fear in all the clowns gathered, especially Silver who shook from head to toe at these words. Alcazar Bezerk The Ringmaster walked in with an easy stride although he carried a slim black cane. His red shirt sparkled devilishly under the lights and threw up a red glow onto his painted face. Silver tried to hide behind some of the other clowns but the ringmaster was quick and reached around the clowns and grabbed her wrist.

"No, no, I just can't do it tonight. I'm still too emotional over what happened last week. I can't do it!" She pleaded as she shrank under his fierce grip.

"Silver, I'm sorry about Roscoe but you can't let that stop us! The show must go on! You're practically our main attraction! And you're going to give it up just like that? Go on, get up on that rope and practice."

"Alcazar I just don't feel safe! Maybe if we put the net back up…"

"Only for practice Silver. You know what those programs say! Why you're the queen of the air! We need you up there confident and proud like you've always been. Just because Roscoe isn't up there with you doesn't make it any different. You know what I say, The Show Must Go On!"

"Oh you and you're fucking show!" Silver cried out suddenly. "That's all you care about. You don't give a damn about us or that we may be heartbroken and terrified! I can't do it tonight don't you see it's just too soon! I can't do it!"

"Damnitt Silver don't make me angry!" The ringleader said although he was already visibly angry with his eyes bulging and his face red with rage. His proud stature hovered over the small clown who stood bravely under him.

"Hey Alcazar give Silver a break. If she's not ready she's not ready. Let her come around in her own time huh?" One of the clowns said as he stood up for her and tried to reason with the ringleader.

Before any one else could react, Alcazar let off and smacked Silver so hard that she was thrown to the ground with the force of the blow. Everyone gasped at this act of violence including me as I hid beneath the bleachers. I had given away my position and one of the clowns came running under there after me. I tried to give chase but he was quick and agile and had me pinned in no time.

"Hey Alcazar look what I got here!" Cried out the clown as I stared up at his smeared face. "It's a little boy!"

"Bring him out!" Cried the big man. I tried to resist and fight back but one clown was quickly joined by two more and their strong hands held me aloft in the air as they walked over to Alcazar and presented me to him for his inspection. One thing I was glad of however was that Silver made good use of the distraction and ran off backstage.

"Well well well." The big man said. He wore a jacket of red sequins that opened to reveal his hairy chest. His head was covered in fine black hair that was slicked back and his face was painted into a perpetually smiling grimace. He was a large man and when he wanted to be he was perfectly terrifying. This was one of those minutes. "Just what were you looking at kid? Trying to get a peek at the circus before its time huh?"

I could only swallow hard and nod in confirmation. The clown's fingers dug into my arms terribly but as I squirmed they only held on tighter.

"And do you like the circus son?" The ringleader asked leaning in real close so I could smell his rancid breath. I nodded yes. "Have you ever seen the circus before?" I nodded yes out of fear of making him angrier. "Do you think you would like to *be in* the circus?" He whispered. I nodded again as my heart pounded high in my throat.

"What should we do with him boss?" Asked one of the clowns that held me.

"Well set him down for right now so he can talk." The clowns released their hold on me and I collapsed to the ground, my knees being too weak to hold me up.

"What's your name boy?"

"Jack." I stammered as I gazed up the length of the man's huge body.

"Jack huh? I'm Alcazar Bezerk the leader of this whole show. Where's your parents, don't they know where you are? I'm sure they would get awfully mad if they found out you were spying on the circus!" The ringleader said as he bent over me.

"I, I, I don't know." I stammered again.

"Stand up and talk to me boy!" He cried out. One of the clowns grabbed my hand and hauled me to my feet while the ringleader crouched down to look at me in the eyes. "Well?"

"I don't have a mum and my dad is in the bar getting drunk." I said with a big breath of air.

The ringleader laughed real big which was echoed by the chuckles of the clowns around us. The ringleader looked around at his cohorts with a gleaming grin. "Well Jack, you know you look mighty dirty for a boy of your age. Doesn't your father bathe ya?"
"Um no, not really." I said as I shook my head.

"Aye! And you look mighty skinny for a boy of your age, how old are ye now?" He took my wrist as if to measure it's thickness.

"Nine."

"Nine, huh doesn't your father feed ya?" "Um sure." I said.

"What did you have for supper last night Jack?"

I stammered as I tried to remember what had been my last meal. I remembered eating discarded circus peanuts and some stale bread I had found in the trash bin. "Bread." I said.

"With nothing on it?" He said.

"No." I said as I shook my head again.

Alcazar shook his head as he dropped my wrist and turned me around to inspect my poor attire. "You're a filthy child son, but it's not your fault. Still a child should not be dressed in rags and eating stale bread every night for supper. You need a change and I'll tell you what it is. You need a mother to feed ya and bathe ye in the tub. You need a father who will teach ya and spoil ya wit love. You need some brothers who will dress you right so's ya can flirt with all zee girls! And you need some sisters who will tease ya and dress you down with pearls! What you need my boy is a new family, one that can treat you right. And this might just be your lucky day cause boy you look a fright. But we just happen to have an opening in our troupe for a child such as you. All you need is to learn some tricks and you'll be good to go. Soon girls will fawn over you wherever ye may go.

"My son you'll live the circus night and day! For there's always another show! You'll see the world and all that's in it and in every town we go, the people will call out to you for more and more and more! There's always something else that's new for the people who are bored. Come with me son and you'll be the envy of every boy and girl, who wishes that they could join us too and run off with the show. But this is a special offer that I make to only you. For our circus needs something that's bright and young and new. And today just may be your lucky day cause that something new is you!" The ringmaster had taken to prancing around as he finished his lines to me and the clowns all applauded with glee as he bowed down low in front of me and offered me his slim cane.

"Take it." Whispered the clown at my back. So I took the proffered cane from his hand and smiled as the ringmaster smiled back at me.

The ringmaster jumped up and cried. "That does it. I'll take care of the rest, just tell me you're father's name Jack."

I told him his name and Alcazar snatched the cane back from my startled hands. "Ex-cell-an-tae!" He exclaimed drawing out each syllable. "I'm going for a walk now, boys take care of young Jack. It looks like he could use a meal from the mess and perhaps a new dress. And teach him a thing or two while you are at it." He walked out but just before he was gone he turned and said one more thing. "Why don't you teach him the giant swing! That should be good for him!"

The clowns voiced their approval and as suddenly as the ringmaster had appeared he was gone.

That day I just hung out with the clowns who showed me such things that up to that point in my nine years of life I could have never imagined on my own. They dressed me in a wonderful jumpsuit of poka-dots with a big puffy collar of the softest material I have ever touched. They showed me some of their circus tricks like juggling and knife throwing and tumbling. They showed me their tiny car and how most of them can fit in it. After twelve clowns had piled into the tiny thing, they cried out for me to jump in. I didn't see how there was room but they pulled me on top of them and then laughed gleefully as they piled out on top of each other with me on the bottom of the pile. They all introduced themselves to me and fed me lunch and treated me so wonderfully that I began to hope that the ringmaster was serious about what he had said.

Later that afternoon, Silver came out and practiced on a tightrope with a net under it while two clowns coached and encouraged her from the ground and two other walkers raced up and down and danced about the ropes with her. Halfway through practice she fell with a scream which startled the other walkers so that they dropped to hang onto the shaking rope. Silver screamed as she climbed out of the netting saying she wasn't ready, she wasn't ready. None of the clowns said a word as the other walkers climbed down to comfort her. In a few minutes, they all got back up and tried the trick over and finished their routine.

"Her husband just died what a week ago." Jasa the clown told me. "He was run over by one of the circus rigs. Those big trucks we haul our stuff around in. Well somehow, he got underneath one of them and it cut him up real good. Silver's been real upset and has refused to do her act. Well that makes old Alcazar real mad cause the most important thing to him is putting on a good show no matter what it takes. Remember that kid. If it's between you and the show don't expect it to come out in your favor."

The clowns didn't wait for them to finish; instead they took me around to see all the animals that the circus had. Two big elephants Titus and Rasha, two spotted leopards Dot and Spot, a pack of small poodle dogs who barked and barked till I petted their soft heads. And lastly, they showed me the big lion Mother Africa, who paced back and forth in her trailer and growled at us as she showed off her big teeth. "Never get in the lion tamer's way." The clowns told me. "He has a worse temper than Mother Africa herself and if you make him mad he might chop you up and feed you to his pet for dinner." Jasa, who told me this, had a slight smile on his lips but I thought it best not to test his words as his smile could just be painted on like the rest of his face.

By the time the ringleader returned, the circus had just enough time to eat the dinner that Cobos the Hobo clown had made and get ready for the show. I was served a big plate of rice and beans with peppers and tomatoes on top and a slice of buttered bread. The beans were so spicy that I could barely eat them although I was so hungry I certainly tried! I sat on the side of the ring between Jasa and Alcazar who laughed at me when my face turned red and my eyes watered from the spicy food. Halfway through the meal, Alcazar stood and called for everyone's attention.

"Tonight, I would like to introduce Jack to all of you!" He cried and as I stood the clowns and artists oohhed and awwed for me. "He is now officially part of the circus!" He told everyone. "I had a lovely chat with his father today who agreed to sell young Jack to us for a very reasonable offer. I hope you all help take care of our newest child and teach him all he wants to know. I see much potential in this boy who represents the future of the circus! To the show!" He cried and lifted his goblet of wine.

"To the show!" Echoed the whole entourage as they toasted and laughed.

"Tonight, young Jack is going to perform on the giant swing near the end of the show. Right Jasa?" Alcazar announced.

Jasa nodded uncomfortably as he had forgotten to show me anything about the 'giant swing'. Alcazar went on for a few more minutes congratulating everyone on the previous show the night before and then critiquing the performers on how they could do better tonight.

The rest of the clowns and circus artists scarfed down their food as they passed around several loaves of bread and big bottles of red wine that they quickly emptied. When they were finished eating, they turned their plates in to the kitchen and retreated to their respective trailers to ready themselves for the show…

All too soon, the day was over and it was time for the entertainment of the night. I watched in awe from backstage as the big top swelled to the rafters with people of all types. Adults with multicolored hair toting crying and gleaming children behind them. Soon the masses grew too big to pick out the individual people as the rich mingled with the poor in their seats under the big top. Smokey the clown sat me on a stool backstage and offered me his joint. The first time I had ever smoked the pungent smoke, which made me cough terribly. All to the smug amusement of the clown. He bid me to take 'another toke' then patted me on the back as he walked away telling me to sit tight and enjoy 'the best seat in the house'. "This is where you get to see how it all happens!" He told me with a toothless grin. I sat there silently through the whole show slightly uncomfortable due to the strange harness the clowns had strapped me into for the 'giant swing'. The only instruction I got was that they would come for me when it was time and I was simply to spread out my hands and feet and smile.

It all started innocently and magically. Alcazar Bezerk The Ringmaster stood alone on a darkened stage and the crowd hushed expectantly. As the music grew mysteriously, a lighted ball about the size of a head appeared in the ringmaster's hand. Magically he danced it around his body, lighting his features as it rolled down his arms and around his head in a mesmerizing manner. Slowly the lights came up and he added another ball to the mysterious beauty of his contact juggling. The first and best

juggler of the kind I had ever or would ever see. As he finished his routine, he welcomed the audience to the show and told them to prepare themselves to be amazed. Then he threw the balls high into the air where they disappeared. The crowd cheered wildly as a lithe assistant walked out with a rack of large knives. With great aplomb and hype, he swallowed first a small sword and then a larger one. As I watched from backstage, I remember thinking that to this there was no trick, those massive blades were straight and strong and reached clear down to the bottom of his stomach!
With a cry, he pulled the last blade out of his gullet and announced the next act.

    The lights came on and the music soared into a cacophony of swirling noise as the clowns came out in their miniature car. Driving around in circles as one by one they climbed out till thirteen of them were prancing about the stage. They threw knives at each other and just as the clown throwing knives threw the last one, the clown who had been standing as the target moved out of the way as the blade whistled straight for the spot where his head had been. The clowns bullied themselves around then started juggling fire sticks tossing them back and forth to each other with great speed and accuracy. Various clowns jumping in and out of the stunts with practiced ease. Then they tumbled through hoops and over seesaws enticing all the time great fits of laughter that roared forth from the huge audience. For their finally, they lit the hoops on fire and jumped through them. The last clown to go through acted very scared and hit the ring on his way to the ground. Suddenly his entire body was on flames! He ran about flailing for a minute then the others put him out with fire extinguishers. Then to the delight of the audience, he rolled about and jumped around to show that he was ok as the hall erupted with applause.

    Then came the animals. First the elephants pranced about the stage, holding lovely women in their trunks and performing handstands and trunk-stands. They seemed transformed from the drab creatures I had seen earlier that day due to the bright dresses of feathers and sequins that decorated their heads and bodies.

From there, the leopards and lion came out in a quickly erected fenced area in the center of the stage which the elephants had helped drag in. The leopards jumped over each other and through big hoops and then laid down for the tamer who carefully walked atop of them! Meanwhile the lion roared and roared from her separate cage to the side till the tamer put the leopards in their side pin and released the lion. She leaped out and pounced upon the wire mesh of the leopards' cage in jealous rage. The leopards roared back as the tamer quickly attended the lion and somehow calmed her down to do his bidding. He ended the routine by placing his head in her mouth after which she let out another loud roar. The tamer jumped back to the applause and cheers of the crowd then exited the stage with his big cats.

Amongst these spectacular feats of skill and daring were many other wonders too numerous to describe them all. Such is the magic of the circus which aims to spellbind and enchant all who pay the small fee to enter the land of the big top. For one night, the viewer is transformed to a realm where the impossible happens. The laws of gravity do not exist here in the same manner as the outside world, nor do laws of nature where the animal tamers bend the will of their terrifying beasts to his own. The lights lead the eyes through the actions of the performers as the music leads the heart to wild and new dreams. Such heart and dedication that is poured forth from the performers every night in different cities as they travel are not rewarded with piles of riches and money. No to the circus performer the real treasure and reward is the love and applause they entice from the masses. Such is the nature of the circus and when a performer doesn't have his heart in his work it shows in his performance.

Thus, as the night drew on, it finally came time for the tightrope act. As the lights dim, the ringleader walks out in a single spotlight to announce the next act. "'Silver, the Queen of the Air' and her prince and princess Lark and Aria! Watch closely ladies and gentlemen as they defy gravity and dance for you in midair without the security of a net! Truly one of the greatest wonders to be seen under the big top as they walk the tightrope with skill and ease. Please no photography and if you will, give us your complete silence till the end of the show! Oh yes, and don't try this at home kids."

The spotlight followed Lark as he took the lead and pranced up the slanted rope to the platform high, high in the air. Then Aria followed behind him in the same prancing dancing manner up, up, up the rope to a great height that seemed to loom even higher the longer I looked. When she reached the platform, Aria took Lark's hand and they bowed to a muffled applause from a respectful and enthralled audience. Then the light followed Silver as she slowly walked to the taunt rope. She was dressed in a skintight outfit as were the other two, only hers was fancier with more sparkles and designs than the others. She approached the rope and swung around on it a few times as if testing its tension. Then she pulled herself upright and pranced up to the platform to join her peers.

Of their stunts I can say little for fear of not giving them enough justice. To walk across a single line suspended far above and do flips and turns and dances… Such skill and dedication and wonder these people commanded as the air under the top grew thick with suspense and wonder. Some of the clowns joined me to watch from my backstage seat. "Get ready, you're next!" He whispered to me as he showed me the end of a thick rope with a hook in the end. As they walked the rope, he fastened my harness to this rope making me suddenly very nervous and scared.

Still I could barely take my eyes off the wonderful feats as Lark rode a unicycle across the rope then Aria jump-roped on it! After each act the performer would retreat to the platform and raise their hands high while the audience clapped then fell silent for the next stunt. The ringmaster asked for silence once again for this next stunt and not even a baby cried or a man coughed.

The silence was complete.

Carefully, Silver rode the unicycle to the center of the rope with the jump rope in her hand. The single spotlight illuminated her sweaty face as she hopped the rope once, twice…

A crashing thud was heard clearly in the complete silence as the spotlight stood still illuminating the tightrope and nothing else. A gasp rose through the crowd and the clowns by my side cried out. The ringmaster jabbed his cane at me and Jasa the clown. "Go now!" He rasped as he ran out to the center of the black stage with a black blanket.

Alcazar threw the blanket over the crumpled figure on the ground then stepped aside for the spotlight to find him away from the mess. "Have no fear ladies and gentleman, it is all part of the show and you have just witnessed the greatest illusion of all! With that in mind! Have no fear and no regrets for life is strong and The Show Must Go On!"

As if on cue, the band started playing again and my harness was tugged back then I was shoved forward at great speed as I was pulled up into the air. I remembered what Jasa had said about putting my arms out but I fear the vertigo made me flail about wildly as I was blinded by the spotlight following me around. I dimly perceived two to four other clowns swinging about and they grabbed at me laughing and then threw me hurling beyond again, passing me it seemed from one to the other. It was a terrible game and a terrible trick I knew it, for Silver was dead but the ringmaster was covering it up.

As the music died down and the lights came up, the stage was once again clear with only a flat black cloth lying in the spot where Silver had been. "That's it ladies and gentlemen I hope you enjoyed the show! See you next year!" The ringmaster shouted as a stream of clowns and artists poured out from the sides of the stages to bow in unison. I was slowly lowered to the ground amongst their midst and waved when the clowns told me to. The crowd applauded though somewhat reluctantly and then poured out to the streets after we exited back stage.

Behind the curtains the chaos grew too extreme as the concerned performers huddled about the still form of Sliver's body that lay on top of a platform still entangled with the unicycle. The two other walkers bawled right over the corpse and the clowns began to cry despite their painted smiles.

"Silence everyone silence!" Alcazar bawled over the cacophony. "Some of you have to greet the public! But I want not a word of this spoken to them. We can't have so many people back here go!"

With that some of the clowns came outside with me where they greeted the public with their painted smiles. Many of the people looked sad and worried and tried asking about Silver but the clowns only said 'they couldn't tell now if she would be all right but probably she would be ok.' I recognized some of my old friends and said hello to them although only my best friend Ben recognized me. I told him I was going away with the circus and to tell everyone goodbye for me. I scanned the crowds till they dwindled to almost nothing for another sight of my father who I knew I would never see again but he never showed up.

That night Jasa let me sleep in his trailer with him and when I woke up the next morning, the circus was almost completely packed and ready to move on. I ran to my father's shack to tell him goodbye but he was not there. When I started running for the bars, I was intercepted by Jasa who had been searching for me. "There you are you little pipsqueak." He cried as he found me. "We've been looking all over for you, come on we're leaving town now."

"But my father!" I protested. "I've got to say goodbye!"

"He already knows kid. Besides we're your family now. I know it will be hard but soon you will love us more than you ever loved your dad. I know because I've been there. Come on now! We don't want to miss the circus train!" With that we returned to the empty field where the big top had stood previously. It was late afternoon and everyone was ready to go on to the next town and the next show.

Shortly after, I began to practice with the tight-rope-walkers who taught me patiently everything they knew over time. When it was time to pick a stage name, it was Aria who suggested Silvan in Silver's honor since I came into the circus the day she died. I took it and it's been my name ever since. Still even after I had mastered the ropes, I could never bring myself to stop clowning. You see that's something about clowns that most people don't know. It's all an act. The happy faces and the makeup and the goofing around. For as I got to know them, I realized that most all the clowns had deep hurt that they covered up with all that makeup and the big noses. And sometimes when we traveled people would be very mean to us clowns because we were so weird.

I don't know if the pain will ever truly fade for the loss of my true father and my childhood. Or for the loss of my true mentor who died the same day I met her. Still it is as they say. The show must go on.

Cirkus Theme Song
Pandemonium, Pandemonium, Pandemonium, Pandemonium

We'll take your children we'll
take your dreams we'll take your
nightmares and make them real!
We'll take your money we'll take your drugs we'll take the things that you call love!

Pandemonium, Pandemonium, Pandemonium, Pandemonium Pan's Demons, Pan's Demons, Pan's Demons, Pandemonium! The Fairies are hiding way up in the trees, they throw down upon you the silliest of things! You think it's all funny until you can see, what they have hidden inside of your dreams. Daydreams erupt like kaleidoscope scenes reality is seldom quite what it seems!

Pandemonium, Pandemonium, Pandemonium, Pandemonium Pan's Demons, Pan's Demons, Pan's Demons, Pandemonium! The Demons are running away with the show they'll chase you until there is nowhere to go your lying and dying and crying and dead! only to find it was all in your head the clowns were not laughing when the mime spit the tale that there's many way in, But None out of HELL!

Pandemonium, Pandemonium, Pandemonium, Pandemonium Pan's Demons, Pan's Demons, Pan's Demons, Pandemonium! So on with the show, away with the show the day of the show it must go on with the show, away with the show the day of the show it must go on with the show, away with the show the day of the show it must go on!

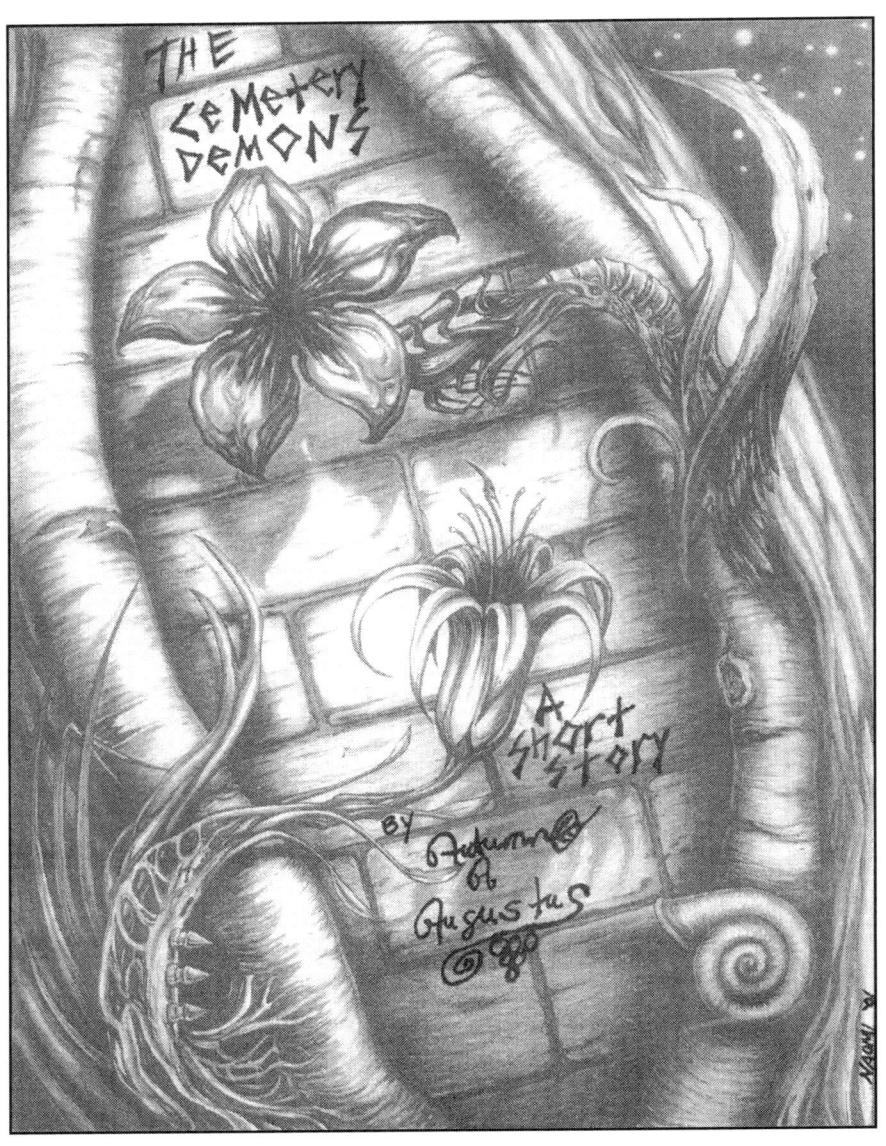

Illustration By Naomie Seraphina

The Cemetery Demons
Autumn '00

When it comes to finding my way around, I pride myself on two things; my good sense of direction and my equally strong sense of adventure. I had been looking for a room to rent for far too long in this city. My canine companion Arkaia and I had found ourselves outliving our welcome on a comfortable couch we had been enjoying for the first few months of our stay in Portland Or. So one late November evening with blessedly full stomachs and a full backpack, we hit the road to make ourselves scarce in what was quickly becoming a tumultuous domestic situation.

To this date, I still do not know the destiny that called me up to the city of Portland, but I can still hear the call for attention that blows in with the wind on the high tree tops. Making them sway back and forth in an exciting clatter of gossiping leaves. If one listens closely enough, one can hear the message portrayed among the rattling leaves. Many times, it seems, the trees gossip about growing cities and starving animals, acid rain and of course the weather.

But for me, the wind seemed to carry a special message. "Come up North!" the leaves would rattle at me from deep within the old south of Louisiana where I had been living and traveling in a Volkswagen camper van. "Come and play and we will teach you new songs."

So, blindly, I set out in an aging vehicle older than myself. "Where do I stop?" I ask the wind.

"We will let you know." Came a wise knowing voice. So, when my ride of summer fun and festivals halted and brought me to Portland with a blown engine, I felt I should stay and see what this city had to offer me.

"Ok, I'm here." I tell the fairy rings.

"Then come dance and play." Chatter the rustling leaves as a storm front begins to move in. I hear a mirthless laughter taunting me to seek out the source.

So, thusly denied of a roof for the night, I resigned myself to a good soaking of the cool northerly rain and hopefully a good romping through the forest in the process.

Where to? Where to? Where to? Quickly I feel a pulling at my heart centers as if a beacon cries to my soul. I follow it down unknown neighborhood streets with a skip in my steps as I follow my merry pup Arkaia. As the night wears on, I pass countless houses. Quiet yards and stray cats catch the attention of my familiar while I gaze up at the eerie TV blue lighted windows and slow moving shadows that pass the curtains without a glance outside. I wonder at the marvels of the modern-comfort-home that swallows the time and lives of those inside.

I feel a compulsion to turn this corner and then the next. Making a zigzag pattern through the city. We play in the shadows of the streetlights as cars silently hiss by in the growing drizzle of rain. Ahead I hear the laughter of a house party and as we sneak upon the scene, we see a gaggle of subdued revelry. The party stays inside while the light and noise spill out to the street like a beacon. Although I do not stay to even mingle, I do pause to discreetly pick up a mostly full cocktail sitting on a window ledge. With a short whistle, I'm joined by my familiar and we stealthily steal away drink in hand without a glance back at the last mortals I was to see that evening.

After a short pause to consume my stolen bounty, I leave the glass as a gift on a random doorstep and continue in the direction of this silent call that beckons me into the stilling darkness.

I skip ahead on the sidewalk and come abruptly to a rock wall that's as high as my chest, lined with a chain-linked fence and topped with formidable barbed wire. "Can we go in? Can we go in?" My familiar asks with bouncing bunny hops that convey her excitement at the prospect of romping through the grass and silently chasing squirrels up trees. A nervous rustle rises in my stomach as I look upon the tall pillars erupting sporadically out of the ordered rows of plots. The soft rain makes pattering noises, which beckon me into the cemetery.

"We'll see." I say as I move along the tall fence. 'Why do cemeteries have fences? ...Because people are dying to get in!' Ha the old joke pokes through my thoughts just as I spot a hole along the bottom of the fence. It was so high on the rock wall however that I had to pass it by because although I could have made the climb, I would have had to lift my girl up though it which would make it a difficult task. I took note of this escape route and looked for another entrance.

Around the corner and down the street some, I find what I'm looking for. The back gate had a space in it that my familiar could fit through while I climbed over the bare chain-link. Let me say now that I have always felt some affinity towards cemeteries thus felt no fear on this wet cold night. My plan was to find a good place in these grounds to lie down, put my dog on her leash and fetch some sleep. What happened on this eventful night, turned out to be quite the opposite of what I had ever dreamed. . .

When I jumped to the other side of the gate, I immediately perceived a veil of energy enveloping the whole grounds like a thin electric red fog. This type of energy I had felt in only one other cemetery in New Orleans where I saw the portals of the West Gate yawn open during a lunar eclipse. But even here this energy was different...

At any rate, when we entered the grounds my familiar was off chasing some squirrels and shadows I know not which. I leaped after her through the thick carpet of leaves that were so damp that our passage made such little noise that the rain easily covered it up. As we ran, I suddenly stopped in front of a very unusual tree. It had a darker aura than most everything else, almost as if it were the source of the strange energy I felt. But that was not what made the tree stand out for it had at one time somehow split down the center creating a very wide gap in the trunk that had been bricked up! A portal! To where?

Leaning in for a closer examination, I noticed firstly that it seemed to be bricked from the inside for the trunk made a large lip around the aperture from years of growth. Secondly, as I examined the bricks, I couldn't help but notice that one was very loose. I couldn't resist the temptation, so I gave it first a good pull, which moved the brick out about an inch, and then a good push. To my astonishment, the brick slipped through! I didn't hear it land inside the tree, but was awed at the red-green glow that came from within. I put my hand in to see what I could feel which was nothing. Looking in I saw only blackness although a cold musty breeze blew out from the deep recesses of the underworld.

What happened next really made my skin crawl and brought about the first stirrings of fear I would feel that night. A bright lightning bolt lit the sky with a growling crack of thunder to accompany it. This thunder made such a horrible sound that I had ever heard and birthed a second growing growl from within the dark depths of the earth under the violated portal tree.

I had a vision of a beast crawling up towards me so I stuffed a handful of leaves in the hole while commanding the unknown to back off. I called to my familiar and went running to look for some sort of shelter against the pouring rain.

"There are no angels in this cemetery." I stated out loud. "Who cares for the dead here and keeps out the demons?" Just as I finished this statement, my long skirt caught me by some clipped rose branches. Cursing I ripped them away which caused me to prick my finger and draw blood and rip my skirt in the process. "Now you've done it!" I said. "Fuck." Then, looking behind me, I saw a lurking shadow move from one grave marker to the next. Startled, I resumed my run deeper into the cemetery.

As it was a late November evening, there were pumpkins still scattered about. One of which I tripped over in my blind haste! Looking up from the ground where I had fallen, I found myself staring at a pair of cast feet topping a grave. The only remains of the angel that had undoubtedly once adorned this site and had since been ripped off. In a flash of lighting I read the inscription that burned its image into my mind. "Daughter of F.O. and L.B. Smith, Born April 22 1879 Died Feb 11, 1885. 5 years old, I thought, the only angel that once adorned this spot is gone. It's as if the cemetery spirits wanted me to see the remains of their last angel placed there over a hundred years ago.

The next crack of thunder struck so close that it shook the earth. The lightning hit a tree and shadows leapt fearsomely alive as flames took to the tree. I looked to the fire and saw such a creature that could never come naturally out of this world! It's crooked stance and leaping gait were enough to tell me that it was monstrous. My heart leaped through my chest as fear for my life shook my soul. A filthy preternatural glow illuminated the gnarly hair and spike tipped bones along the back of the beast. My dog with shackles raised growled bravely at it till it rose to a fearsome height and hurled a hellish roar at the night. I promptly took to my heels taking my dog's collar as she ran to my side.

Darting among trees and gravestones the hellish demon chased us almost playfully like a cat chasing mice in a field. Reaching into the pocket of my leather jacket, I pulled out what I first grasped an assortment of crystals and stones I had wrapped in silver for talismans. Breaking the hemp they were tied upon, I hurled first a large rose quartz at the creature as it prowled slowly upon us. The charmed crystal hit the beast on the forehead directly above its glowing red eyes that gave off such light that the demons breath was glowing with the evil color. The blow of the magic rock seared a brand into the forehead over its third eye and I heard the hissing of burning flesh over its angry snarls.

Momentarily delaying its pursuit of us, I yanked my dog into movement who in turn added to our momentum from the beast. We could not run fast enough though, and as I felt the putrid breath of the beast upon my back I neared yet another portal. This one was formed by four evenly spaced redwood trees in a square giving off a faint shimmer between the majestic trunks. Ready to overtake me, I threw the remaining handful of talismans including a large bell at the beast. Because of his closeness, most of them hit and sunk magically into the flesh of the creature burning its chest and face and causing the demon to collapse and roll violently on the ground while plucking the silver-wrapped stones from its body.

Only steps away from the portal at this point I yanked my dog through and she landed on top of me as I landed on a very hard tombstone, breaking it in three pieces. The top piece had an inscription of a strange archaic symbol that I had never seen before and pressed its image into the back of my hand where it would remain for a few days in the form of a bruise.

As we collected ourselves, so did the demon who began pacing in front of us outside of the portal. The monstrous abolition stopped short of the entrance and leered at me. In its eyes glowed like fires of hell and from its breath came burning acid that smoked on the ground when it's saliva dropped. I had locked gazes with this demon! Not daring to look away and loose power over this unnatural demonic spawn, I held my ground hoping the portal entrance would keep me safe as my instincts told me it should. With my free hand, I fumbled in my pocket for my magical blade known as an athame. As I pulled it out, the demon became distracted by the flash of the jeweled hilt and silver blade and looked at it, breaking first its gaze into my eyes. Realizing it had lost the stare out; it cried in rage and flung itself towards me. I fell backwards flinching at its advance at the same instant that it hit the east portal entrance. Bouncing off an energy shield with an electric burst that threw it onto its back.

I on the other hand fell through the opposing westerly 'doorway' of the sanctuary dragging my familiar with me. My right leg went numb as it lay on the threshold of the different dimensions and as I removed it took some time to wear off. While standing, I clipped on my familiar's leash and found myself in bright daylight. No thunderstorm, no demon. I immediately realized I was in another dimension as it were.

* * * *

Ahead of me, I discerned a strange cacophony of still unearthly yet familiar musical sounds. With my leashed familiar I ventured forward. Almost at the same instant we saw each other, I crested a small hill.

"Halt!" Cried the Queen of this fairy band for Queen she defiantly was. Her entire body shimmered iridescently royal purple. Her gown was of a material so fine it could have been made of spider silk. Her bodice was tightly fitted and she wore fishnet like sleeves that flayed out at the wrists like strange flowers that accentuated her long and pointy hand and nails of a dark shadowed hue. Her skirts hung in fine multihued colors hiding her presumably pointed feet, which hovered slightly off the ground. Her skin was blue as the cloudless sky and her hair was black as a starless night.

Behind her was a large group of shimmering fairies. The myriad band of musicians and dancers froze in midair halting their cacophonous cavorting and playing. Slowly as one, they all turned to stare. Letting their banjos, harps and flutes hang there.

The Queen rose on barely perceptible shimmering wings and moved swiftly through her charges to stop abruptly in front of me.

"Who are ye that dare
enter my sanctuary
where no gifts shall be
rare but all must pay a
fare?"

Her voice echoed strangely in my ears like the ringing of many bells and it took great effort to remember my manors. I curtsied hiding my athame in the folds of my skirt. "I am Autumn Augustus your majesty and this is my familiar Arkaia." I realized I was again caught in a locking gaze with eyes that hinted of many treasures in their solid black depths lined with irises of rainbow. She seemed to read right through me with her stern feathery soul.

"Have ye brought this beast to
become our feast?"

A jingle of laughter broke out after this and I lost the stare to look at the crowd of elves and fairies gathered in this unusual place. A bit flustered I replied, "Oh no your majesty. This is my familiar, and she is my most cherished companion. I didn't mean to disturb you. I can leave again, it's just this awful demon was chasing me and I stepped in the middle of the four trees where it couldn't come and I went out the other side and ended up here."

"Our meeting is not by chance, ye
shall join our dance become
enthralled by our romance we are
fairies of the Fae we will dance
with ye all day and then send thee
on thy way our bidding we shall ask
and then send thee on a task
come drink now from my flask."

She held out to me a delicate cup of lily pedals and fine silken thread that held sweet nectar. Feeling myself in great danger my intuition told me to run but I could not. The smile of the Queen was so kind and the nectar of the flowers so sweet. As I first sipped the sweet juice, the band of pipers started playing again. The

Queen urged me to drink it all so I did, savoring its bitter sweetness and the tingle it gave my tongue. I barely felt the little hands tug the leash out of my hand to lead my dog away.

They had both of us enthralled and I watched with a detached care as little fairies each about a foot in height tied up my dog to a grave stone and then began to tease and play with her while others tugged at my skirts and began to spin me in circles leading into a ring they formed around a large tree. The tree had a plaque on it which they lead me to read. "The original tree for which Lone Fir Cemetery was named 1866 The pioneer rose association February 14, 1939."

Tightly little hands and claws clung to my hands, feet and dread locked hair pulling me about like a marionette around the tree in three big circles, spinning like a top the whole way around, around, around.

The fairies laughing all the way.

Suddenly the music took an abrupt halt, ending in a wilting wallowing flute. I felt my body wobble softly. Gazing down I saw the ground far below my feet, one booted, the other clad only in a clammy sock. The fairies receded in a rainbow of flashing colors to take position in a circle leaving me levitating on my own in the air, the wind blowing softly around me and through me! Strangely yet beautifully illuminated was my Fairy Queen as the crowd of fairies parted dropping flower petals on the earth before her. So fully enchanted with her mysterious beauty this Queen had me. I caught nary a glimpse of the other performers as the Queen embraced me in her stick like arms and started up the dance again. Taking me mercilessly in endless spirals and stars. Yet we disturbed none of the fallen petals which lay colorfully under my floating feet.

She smelled like heady mushrooms and her blue skin felt like soft silk except where her hands grew into sharp twigs lined with little thorns. She sang with an indescribable voice that echoed and bounced along my brain.

Time was lost as I was carried away by the music of the fey. Catching glances here and there of my surroundings over her small delicate shoulder. I saw that my pet was also enthralled by the terrible sprites who were scratching her belly non-stop. Paralyzing all but her wildly beating leg much to the amusement of her tormenters.

Through the heavens my Faire Queen took me among the clouds lit with spectacular rays of sun. A hoard of wildly clad winged fairy folk accompanied us, some dressed in scraps of fabric others in spider silk and autumn leaves, all echoing the chants of the queen or playing their infectious music. The twisted rhymes and lopsided meter of her songs I cannot recall, nor even their message for she had me securely spell bound and charged me to carry out duties of which nature I am not sure although the writing down of these events seem to be one of her many tasks she charged me with.

Suddenly, a disturbance below us caught my stolen attention and broke into the endless spell castings. Somehow my familiar had broken free of her rapture and was chasing the fairy folk around, scattering the cacophonous band into the trees and bushes with shrieks and yells punctuated by her shrill ear piercing barking.

The Queen and I both stopped our wild dance, and realizing I still held my gleaming jeweled athame in my hand, I slashed down on her wrist, breaking our cosmic connection with the shedding of her fairy blood that oozed out of her arm in a thick green sap. From the top of the firtree I fell. Crashing through branches and limbs until my leather jacket caught a substantial branch. For a few precious seconds, I hung there staring down at the fairies on the ground who were staring up at me in astonished silence. Then my jacket ripped and the branch broke as the queen let out a shout of frustration. I crashed unceremoniously to the ground.

The Queen fluttered in front of my face seeming very small and delicate now as she brandished a many faceted crystal wand at me. "As I have sang, and danced this plea and shown my lovely world to thee so be it so mote it be."

I felt a strong current of electricity flow through my body making me tingly and light headed and quite dazed. My familiar jumped to my side to lick my face in her anxious manner. She placed her rope leash in my hand with her mouth and then began pulling away from the mysterious scene.

In my fall from the tree, I had dropped my athame and as I sat up, I saw three pixies fly to it and pick it up. One was very small and delicate with pink translucent wings, her limbs like green blades of grass wearing a tunic of torn colored leaves her hair was a wild thrash of hair that left trails of sparkles behind. The second pixie was a plump purple little thing with thick moth-like wings that fluttered slowly through the air. The third and last was old appearing with long gray locks that tangled in her blinking wings, her gown was made of thick gray webbing that left wisps of silk behind. They picked up my athame, which seemed a hefty burden between the three of them, flew off into the dusky air and vanished right before my eyes. I took the hint of my familiar and let her pull me from the area, sensing that the fairy band was disbanding also in the fading light.

The doorway between the four trees that I had come from was lit with a yellow glow and we headed back into the small grove. As we headed away, the snarling fairies and sprites were pelting us with acorns and twigs and chittering excitedly. The terrible cackling laughter of the beautiful queen beating into the back of my skull, until we were engulfed by the silence and stillness of the magical portal.

* * * *

in the portal, I fell to the ground and clutched the stone headrest in the center and threw up all the food in my stomach. I looked idly at the head stone and read it again. Daniel Wright Born in Pepperell Mass. Jan 29 1814 Died Sep. 2 1873.

As I was recovering my senses, my dog chased some scurrying thing out of the south-facing portal. I saw the shimmering in the reality as she passed through it and vanished from sight amongst the tombstones and trees. "Arkaia come back!" I vainly cried but she did not could not hear me. I stepped out of the treed doorway and was instantly assailed by a strong wind that howled through the tall trees and lifted the fallen leaves in great dancing eddies. I looked for my dog but she was no-where within sight. The sky was filled with silent clouds and glowed faintly in anticipation of the coming dawn. Many of the plots had flowers set upon them and down the hill I heard a whistling piper playing sporadically between fits of giggling laughter. Hugging my leather jacket to my body I limped with one bare foot and one booted down the hill.

Perched atop a tall tombstone on hoofed feet sat a curious piper. His current source of entertainment was my dog who was jumping around while leaping and yapping after the infernal creature as he played a penny whistle and bounced to the music. His thick legs that ended in goat-like hooves were clad in camouflage cargo pants and despite the chill wind, his stout torso was bare and strong. His head was covered in thick brown hair that hung past the middle of his back and his bearded face was humanlike despite the wide grin and the knobby horns that rose from his forehead. He led my dog on a merry chase as he leaped laughingly from one tombstone to the next stopping to gain his balance and pipe out shrill notes of mirth. Engrossed in the game, he did not notice me till my dog ran to greet me.

This Panigiree stopped his piping and looked at me in surprise.
"Who is this pretty you have brought to me? My pleasure to meet thee
Oh, come and play with me."

He addressed my dog first who stood in front of me protectively. Again, I curtsied before I spoke to him. "My name is Autumn Augustus and this is my familiar Arkaia. Really all I want is to find my way out of this haunted place."

"A way out you seek this place
has no leak.
You are such a lovely thing Why don't we go have a fling?
This land is full of magic
And you know it would be tragic
To leave the land of plenty
To find your hands are empty."

Although I found this creature fascinating and curious, I had had my fill of the bizarre for one night, I turned to leave. "Come Arkaia lets go." She bounded ahead of me a few leaps and barked at the Panigiree in surprise as he materialized in front of me with his arms barred across his firm chest.
"You cannot leave stay here with me see all that there is to see."
With that he took my hand and pulled me away from the portal whence I had come.
"In this very cemetery grow so many ancient trees. Each one has been selected very carefully for it's seed. Come along dear and we shall see a
very special creed."

As we approached the old stone crypt, I felt yet another pang of dread. Its simple gothic construction with tall chimney topped with modest crosses matched the colors of the sky, a dismal graying peachy color. It had four simple pillars one on each side and lovely stained glass windows. We approached from the west looking at a barred plywood door on the small 20' by 20' building. Only half of the family name remained banner-like above the doorway reading only MACL. He dragged me up some short steps and around the sidewalk to the front of the building. The door was boarded up with plywood but that didn't stop him. The Panigiree chanted rhythmically.

"What you see is not what you believe. This world you shall leave and come inside with me." He tugged smartly on my arm pulling me through the solid boarded door and we were inside the small shrine room. But it was like no shrine I had ever seen. The dirty stained glass windows let in very little light so the demon caused a small flame on his fingertip with which he lit a few black candles. As the room lit my horror grew. On the large cross above the altar hung an actual body wrapped in the pleated lining of a coffin

like a toga. The stench
was close to unbearable
and as I watched worms
and maggots crawled out
of the empty staring eye
sockets and in and out of
the broken ribcage to
gnaw on the greenish
brown flesh. Below his
crumbling toes was an
altar made of human
limbs.
Even the candles he lit were made of human hands!
    Realizing my imminent danger, I ran into the door not through it as I had hoped I might.

"Do not try to flee you are
trapped here with me. You
are now considered mine and
in this temple, I shall dine! A
nice addition you shall be
when I can love you
eternally."

    He lunged for me barring his pointy teeth and I ducked down and pulled out my deck of tarot cards, which I always carried in my lapel pocket. Thinking quickly, I came up with a rhyme of my own.

"Before we start the romance
Let us play a game of chance We
shall play a game of cards You will
not find it hard."

He sat back and analyzed me quickly. Knowing that betting is any devil's weakness I knew he could not resist. I only hoped that my trusty tarot cards would read in my favor.

"A game of chance is what you say
I'm a player let's play away
Tell me the rules so I will know
When I may deal you're killing
blow." To this I replied to him. "This
is a game of power the odds of
which shall be one of us shall
remain in this tower the other will
be set free a witch relies on the rule
of three, three for you and three for
me."

With this I spread my cards fan like in my left hand letting the Panigiree pick three cards first. He pulled them out randomly from the pile and grinned as I also selected three cards from the deck for myself.

We looked at our cards at the same time, and the Panigiree howled and dropped his cards on the ground as if they burnt him. I had the Queen of Swords to indicate me, witty cunning, adventurous and sly. The Five of Cups, which is the life path card, showing the developments and experiences we need to live in our lifetimes. And the third was the tenth trump card The Wheel which is a sign of good fortune and also give us the chance to open new 'doorways' of opportunity for ourselves. The Panigiree was on his knees rocking back and forth with an evil sheen of hatred in his eyes, he howled first then yelled at me.

"I can't change
I can't change
You little witch
You little bitch

Tell me what these cards say Tell me
tell me right away.

    The Panigiree growled as I looked at his cards and grinned. They were The Tower, the card of self-destruction and hardship. The Hanged Man showing how he was trapped in the tower for he can't indeed change for he was The Fool, the zero-trump card, and I had tricked him. As I began to answer him I felt my feet slowly sinking though the solid brick floor into the room below.

"You are trapped and I am free that is
what the cards do see."
    At this the half-goat man became enraged and leaped at my sinking form.
"Of all the filthy foolish schemes!
Give me those damn pesterous things
Those cards are fixed like angel wings
I shall feed them to my shredding machines!"

    He ripped the deck of cards out of my hand making them fly about the place like trapped birds. I saw his huge filthy claw rake for my head just as I sank into the room below. I managed to hold onto only two cards, The Wheel and The Queen of Swords.
    In the first level of this terrible crypt is the family vault dedicated to the Kerr family. Much of the family is there; Abel, Thomas, Marsha, Roderic, and Tomas Kerr III. The floor space was quite roomy and on the doorway, is a sturdy iron gate locked with a padlock. I rattled the gate helplessly wanting out. "Oh no! Let me out!" At the sound of my voice, my worried pet ran around to the gated door and helplessly wagged her tail as she was happy to see me.
    Calming my sense of panic, I looked about for some way to get out. I noticed that one of the tombstones was lose, so thinking I could try to break the door down I tore off the concrete facing to

one of the crypts to throw it at the gate. When I pried it lose, its cement weight forced itself to the ground with a thud.

"Hello? Is somebody there?" Rang a soft female voice from deep within the crypt.

"Huh?" I looked for the source of the voice but saw only blackness within the deep recesses of the vault. "Hello?" I replied.

Suddenly a strange illumination appeared from the crypt I had just uncovered. Looking in I saw a tunnel that stretched behind the mahogany casket.

"I'm back here in darkness
and fear come and follow
my shout so you can let
me out!"

The voice was so musical and sad and I had nowhere else to go so I obliged. "Arkaia stay there." I told my dog who sat down on the damp cement walk outside the iron gate with an objective whine.

After a little heaving, I could push the casket against the wall leaving barley enough room to crawl by. "Where are you?" I cried as I inched along the damp dark tunnel the smell of wet cement and moldy decay bringing a rise of fear and curiosity to my tight chest. The high voice rang out clearly and echoed off the cement walls.

"Just a little farther dear, you are
getting very near!"

As I passed the casket the ground suddenly sloped up steeply so that I had to brace my feet in the sidewalls just to climb up and the nice square cement tunnel led to a crude earthen grave. At the top I came out in yet another crypt. This one smaller than the first and illuminated only by the single flame atop of the Panigiree's finger! As I entered the room he cackled madly his sharp teeth gleaming in the devilish glow.

"I may be the fool, but I sure tricked you!" He snarled as he lunged at me pulling me into the middle of the small crypt. I had only two weapons in my hand and not much at that. Nevertheless, in desperation I threw an energy blast into the Queen of Swords card and threw it at the sly beast. Just as I had hopped the card cut him up like a hand full of knives. The light went out and I could hear him struggling in the darkness. His breathing grew restless and his words were more and more resembling snarls.

"I am the greatest immortal you will find in this here portal I still do not understand
How you gained the upper hand
Fighting me in my home land
I smell the mark of the fairy queen

Who be it known is very mean
Under her dark enchantment
You have caused my entrapment
But remember this my little sweet
Under freedom's bells revenge will meet."

    These cryptic lines seemed to take a lot out of the Panigiree who was panting heavily when he finished. I on the other hand was looking for the doorway when I felt his cold breath upon my neck and his large hand reach around my waist. The smell of warm musk enveloped me as his voice transformed yet again into soft whispers.

"Oh, won't you sit for one last spell
before you leave me in this hell?" A romp
in the hay is all I ask
It won't take all night to do this task
Lover be and lover see
Lover swoon now over me."

    Feeling myself succumb to his spell I could only ask one thing of him. So, I chanted back my reply feeling the rhymes form themselves as naturally as the rising desire I felt growing within for this magical beast.

"Lover be and lover see won't you be
careful with me Your lust I cannot help
but feel This craving is now very real.
Though you are trapped inside this tower
You have me now under your power.
I will be yours for this one night
But must leave quick upon daylight."
    Oh, how can I next describe the wonderment of what transpired in that small crypt that night? I will attempt but do not

know if it will give the event justice. As he fell upon me in a tight embrace, I asked his name.

"Demon be thee demon I see reveal
thy name right now to me."

"It seems in your head you have nearly
already named me Panigiree,
that will work well for me dearie."

    Soft and hollow were his words that rang out of other worlds. His demonic heady musk seared into my pores, setting ablaze my kundalini fire. Roughly with no foreplay, he wrenched open my skirts and entered my flesh with his massive pulsing member. His roars shook the covers with red flaming light as he bucked me through the air. His massive hands clutching me to his bleeding chest that I had injured. The chill room quickly became an inferno of hellish lust but I could not take off my leather jacket pushed into the corner as I was. Receiving his demonic seed, I orgasmed in paralyzing shudders and gasped for mercy. When he thrust deep inside me, his thrusts turned from frantic to slow and heavy reps making me cry out with each thrust he laughed evilly. He breathed slowly atop me and I could feel my energy pouring from my breath into his form. It became hard to breathe as my breath matched pace with his and his thoughts seemed into my mind as he became stronger and I gradually weaker. "Stop, stop!" I cried as the pain and ecstasy threatened to overcome me but he held me tighter and thrust deeper, his glowing eyes burning in my face, with grunts of pleasure intending to get all he could out of me.

    As I was forced beyond all thresholds of orgasm I had had before or would hereafter experience, I received visions of the hell this creature had come from. Flaming pits of earth surrounded the inhabitants as they fought and loved each other simultaneously constantly searching for an escape from their pain in fits of pleasure. The red-hot fires of hell seemed to reach out to us in our secluded hide away until the walls themselves glowed like hot coals and our dripping sweat sizzled on the floor as it fell. I scratched at the Panigiree's slick back for purchase begged him to stop with what breath I had left.

My body shook uncontrollably beneath him and finally he cried out and shuddered as well. He fell onto his back pulling me on top of him yet still did not release me from his thrusting seed. I raised my head gasping for breath in the boiling room. He caressed my long locks and spoke softly, still moving his hips to a slow steady rhythm.

"Angle you must surely be to
love a beast retched as me."
   "Panigiree you are divine,
   say you'll be forever mine."
"Anything you ask of me your
servant I will gladly be."
   "To come from this tower when I call to thee
   And do all that I can ask of thee." "Angel only tell me what you need for you now carry my demonic seed."   "Anything that I ask you say, stay in this tower under light of day." "You would keep me here in this dark lair away from other mortal's stare?" "Panigiree you are now slave to me, so be it I say so mote it be.   Release your charms off of me."
"As you wish you lovely thing
I shall see you again and my child you'll bring."

He lifted himself off me and turned away in an exhausted heap. Helplessly I slid away on the floor collapsing also into a tired pile. The room was pitch black and still incredibly hot.

"Demon Panigiree I need a light use
your power to make it bright."

    Exhaustedly he raised only his hand and lifted a blazing fingertip. This large playful demonic beast suddenly appeared frail and small his long black hair loose from its ties and scattered about his sweating face. My tarot card was still stuck in his chest like a dagger a small trickle of blood seeping out from it. Gingerly I removed it and discarded it on the floor and taking my winter scarf from the collar of my jacket I wrapped it around his thick hard chest and tied it tight over the bleeding wound with the blessing of a simple healing spell. In my hand was a lock of the Panigeerie's hair that I had apparently pulled free of his head during the throws of ecstasy, this I put in my pocket.
    Looking around the crypt I immediately spotted the covered door of concrete. I touched it to try to pass through it but it gave only resistance. I saw my other tarot card The Wheel on the ground and picked it up and placed it on the doorway. The door lit up softly and my hand began to pass easily through it. Taking one last look at the Panigeerie I said.

"Panigeerie until the next time I call You'll stay
in this tower that is all.
I love you creature of the darkest fall."

    Gingerly I walked through the solid door to find myself once again in the cemetery. By the look of the sky it was early morning and the sun would rise in probably another half-hour as the first rays of light peaked out from over the horizon. I had emerged out of the smaller crypt next to the taller temple. These were the only two crypts in sight amongst the contemporary earthen graves. This red bricked crypt had the same outer plywood door as the other, only now the tarot card of The Wheel was framed in the door. I tried to pull it out but it was magically fixed.

I whistled for my dog who came running to me with her tail between her legs and her leash torn up and dragging on the ground. I gave her a big hug and let her lick at my face between worried whimpers. I rose to leave and started for the front gate when I saw a digging crew enter the cemetery in a truck. I dodged behind a larger stone pillar to watch them park near the front and see two men climb out with shovels. My familiar was growling at them under her breath and I sensed that these were not normal men. And even if they had been, I was in a terribly ragged state to approach them.

Instead we stole away towards the back gate. As we crossed the road, I was looking at an unusual grave toper of a child-sized stone coffin. I walked over it and then immediately crashed into an energy field that would not let me past. I read the grave marker that simply read "With Christ Which Is Much Better." I figured I must be in a different dimension than my own so I ran back to the four-tree portal once again.

* * * *

From the center of those four evenly spaced evergreen trees, I looked out upon four different worlds, each with its own weather and mood. To the east, it was still a pouring rainy night and as I looked the first demon I had encountered was still loose tearing through the grounds, and upon seeing me began a pacing prowl in front of the gateway. To the west, the Sun was still shining and squirrels were chasing each other up and down trees. Black crows gathered in the branches to watch the mysterious working of the mischievous Fay. Behind me to the south glowed a misty dawn and although I had trapped one danger there, I did not want to run into those gravediggers. Which left only one option left, the north. In front of me a thin frost misted the ground and a deep fog hung thickly in the air, hiding any further horrors to come.

"Little pet I think we've been hexed. I don't know what we'll run into next; There's only one way to know, and only one way to go. Let's hope this north-facing door Will give us trouble no more."

My dog followed close to my side as I held tightly to her tattered leash. My heart racing fiercely in fear. Looking around warily in the gloomy sticky fog, I first saw the face of Raisa Denga staring resolutely at me. A stout Jewish woman of 79 years, she had been dead since 2-5-1999 and her ghost waiting above the grave matched exactly with the image etched into her grave stone.

"What's a mortal doing here?" She shrieked at me while she charged at me. This frightened my dog so badly that she pulled me out of her charging way and up the hill in a northeasterly course. This quadrant of the accursed cemetery was teaming with ghosts who apparently did not approve of my trespass. At the cackling howls of the first one, they took after me when I ran past them. The spirits leaped up at us from the frosted earth clawing at my flesh and tearing at my hair.

"A living soul here in the flesh
wearing one shoe beneath her
dress. With nothing to protect her with
She'll soon find out this little witch
That livings hard but deaths a bitch.
You won't escape us dear child
The spirits here are all quite wild.
Hah haha hahahahahhhahahhahahhaha!!!!!!!!
Oooohhhhhhhh oh oh oh oh ohhhhhhh!!!!!!!!

Their shrill shrieks assaulted my ears and infuriated me almost more than their taunting tugs and pulls at our bodies. They gathered around us closing us in their mean circle, chanting, swaying, cackling their nasty rhyme. I was backed into a stone pillar with the family name of Holmes on it. Over a hundred and thirty years dead, this forty-eight year old ghost raced through my chest and then snatched up my dog into the air screaming.

"I'll get you my pretty!
And your little dog too!!!"

Arkaia yelped and tried to bite him but her jaws could not sink into his airy flesh. As the other spirits grabbed at me and tore at my hair, I realized that I did have one magical tool left. My hand closed instantly on the vial of dragons' blood oil in my tattered leather pocket; a potent oil used to anoint sacred space and items, I carried it with me because I use it frequently as a perfume.

Opening the cap with one hand and splashing a bit of the oil onto my hand, I got an instant reaction out of the ghosts closest to me. They backed off a bit and I threw a bit of the smelly liquid on the two closest to me. Their infernal screams of their disintegrating forms haunt me still with shivers of fear for the other side of life. That did not stop me though, it only encouraged me more to attack these aggravated ghosts who would seek to separate me from my familiar. I chanted to him while anointing the ghost and my dog with the dragon oil, ignoring his unearthly screams I attempted to drown them out with my shouting.

"Vile beasts of unearthly power you'll
not defeat me this strange hour. If
you must upon me attack I'll not hold
my defenses back.
Go into the hell from which you came
For fear this world will not be the same."

Writhing in a green oozing agony, this vile looking ghost dropped my dog and fell into a fit of cursing howls as his form was unwillingly pulled into another realm.

I grabbed Arkaia's collar and again took off in a lopping run away from the direction whence I had come. I poured some of the dragon's blood directly onto my familiar's back and held the vile aloft causing the ghosts to part and let us though. The fog became so thick I could not see the ground and cried out in pain when I ran into a stone bench and fell over it, breaking my vile of dragon's blood on the hard stone below.

"Keep your chin up." Read the side of the bench mockingly. Seeing this, the ghosts closed in closer but did not continue their attack. Before moving on, I wiped up some of precious oil and smeared it through my dreadlocks.

Remembering the hole in the fence along the north wall, I picked myself up and, taking my dog's collar in my hand I attempted to keep the spirits off.

"Back away, oh back away back away from me I say lest I call a Panigiree this way
He's under my spell
And he'll send you to h---!!!! "

As I chanted I walked and kept my eyes to the circling ghosts and was cut short as I fell into an open grave! I released my dog's collar as I fell but she still fell in on top of me, bringing the side of the grave wall down with her. It took me a moment to realize what had happened and when I looked up the ghosts were crowding about the top of the six-foot dirt wall throwing dirt and rocks on top of us. All of them cackling at us. I picked up Arkaia and threw her out of the grave and climbed out myself with much effort as I was exhausted and all the strength in my body nearly gone.

As I stood up wearily on the solid lawn, all the ghosts fell back to a respectful three to five feet. I was glad that I had earned that much seeing how I had sent off a few of their companions in style. I was almost to the fence at this point and eagerly searched the wall for my escape route. I glimpsed a dark shadow in the bottom of the fence ahead of me and ran to the hole. I was beaten to my destination however by a foreboding figure of a ghost. His commanding stature stood at the ready with a glowing sword in his hand. I could just make out the hole that led to my freedom between his legs as his voice bellowed above the howling wind.

"This is our land and we've been ordered to protect it
from unholy borders
The bible states thou shall not suffer a witch to live, attack her spirits! This order I give!"

    If these ghosts were really going to destroy me I had no strength left to fight. I pulled out the Panigiree's stolen lock of hair to prepare to call him when to my surprise the other spirits fell not upon me, but on my holy accuser. Several disembodied voices spoke to me at once. "Leave us now, you vile bitch! We shall not fight a powerful witch. Your freedom we will gladly give so that our pasts we may again relive."

    Gladly I dived through the hole feet first landing easily on the ground eight feet below. Then I lifted my faithful companion through after me.

    I had made it out! We were standing there shaken under a rising sun looking behind us into the Lone Fir Cemetery. It appeared a harmless ordinary burial ground from this side of the fence under the first rays of day. No drastic weather changes were visible from this side of the fence and I even spotted a couple of squirrels chasing each other among the flower-topped gravestones.

    Rounding the corner, I found myself at 20th S.E. Morrison in Portland Or. I knew this area although I had not known of that cemetery before last night. Was it last night? It felt as if I had spent days running through that maze. I could not tell the day but I felt terrible and wanted to find some food so I began to walk towards downtown.

I only made it a block when I saw a beautiful dark-haired witchy woman smoking cigarettes on her porch at 1836 S.E. Morrison. I didn't know if I could explain my wild story to her, but she looked friendly enough to talk to and ask for help.

So, with only one shoe, all my magical items gone, my clothes and leather jacket torn, scratches all over, Naomie Serafina took me into her bed and nursed me well with black coffee, tomato soup and second hand smoke. We became good friends instantly.

Miraculously, my dog was relatively unscathed. She had a few shallow scratches presumably from the fairies on her stomach and rips on her ears from the ghosts, but nothing serious.

I tried to convey the incredible events I had gone through over a cup of coffee and breakfast but could only formulate my thoughts into confused lines of jumbled rhymes. Yes, the fairy queen had truly enchanted me.

Naomie only shook her head and told me to rest. She drew me a bath and dressed me in clean clothes before putting me to sleep in her bed while she ran off later than usual to work.

Although I could never really explain the events of that night to her or her roommates, they took me in and let me rent out an extra room there where I lived for about 6 or 7 months. I finally had to move away from the cemetery because of the memories it harbored. Although I'm sure I could love a Panigiree's child that came from my body, I miscarried the little monster very painfully I might add in about the second month of pregnancy.

Gradually the rhyming enchantment wore off and I slowly found my own voice again uninhabited by a fairy tongue. I still do have phases however were upon it takes me again spinning in circles in the blowing wind. Chanting strange rhymes that the fairies did send.

The Portal Tree

Upon the night, fresh and young, to me a cry was sung. Pulling me from my world of light, into a dark and evil night. Attacked by creatures large and small They captured and enraptured me to their call.
A Hell-spawn sprang form a portaled tree.
While the Fairy Queen wooed, and danced with me.
Crafty Panigiree I trapped in his tower
Then defeated a ghost hoard of unearthly power. The portals inside those cursed gates made the weaker and daylight drastically change.
How I escaped I do not know.
But return there, I will not go.

Weeping Willows

Why do the Willows weep?
What kind of secrets do they keep? As the
cold wind blows round
Long leaves reach for the ground.
Why do the shadows creep?
Where the dying often sleep? As
the roses turn around   To
comfort weeping sounds.

Tie a wreath about your hair,
Dance through the willows hanging in air
Sounds of weeping should be saved For
those who lie beneath the grave.

The Willow Weeps for it only knows The stories told when the west wind blows.
But I sing a different song today
For the dead can dance in their own parade.

Illustration By Kip Kelly

The Dance of the Banshees
Winter 2001

Here lies a deserted fishing village on the western coast of Canada. An old ghost town deserted when I was just a young child. For this is where I spent my childhood, in Cape Rock. So named for the large outcropping rock pillar overlooking the cold ocean. The weather here is almost always raining, but when the big storms died down, many of the brave townsmen would go out and haul in their casted nets and lay out more. Although it seemed to be a harsh lifestyle, the bounty of the sea was always rich with large sturgeon and tuna, crabs and lobsters and countless varieties of other fish. We were often cold but rarely hungry.

Why then did this quaint town of stodgy people die off? It is a strange tale and one I saw with my very own eyes as a young child. I've harbored the strange story of Cape Rock in my heart for far too long now in hopes that perhaps someone else would come forth and tell the tale. But I am one of the only survivors and thus I feel it is my duty to tell these events in detail before I am allowed to die. All that is left now are the waterlogged ashes and foundations of this once proud and solitary town.

Coming back here reeks of my childhood. The cold spray of the ocean winds blowing to the east into the land. The sprinkling rain, which feels like a short hiatus in the almost constant pounding storms that put a chill in the bones permanently. I can see the stone walls of the church and next to it the town hall. Scattered about the sorry foundations of houses you will find the rotting carcasses of fishing boats and ancient cars and buggies. We were an old-fashioned type, the women would stay indoors most of the time cooking and making big warm quilts while the men would go out into the vast ocean to fish. A dangerous but rewarding career that supported the entire population of about three hundred people. Entertainment was scarce here as well as education and although many of us were simple folk, the adults were very hard working and honest.

No I am not surprised that I was the last. My mother told me that there was something special about me when I was a child. Something about being protected and watched over. With my green eyes and once stark red hair that stuck out amongst the drab people like a match in a dark room, I would run up to the tops of the rocks and feel wild and free in the blowing wind as it seemed to tell me secrets of the sea. Ah yes, the wind. Wasn't that how it had started? Yes, so clearly, I remember...

It was right around the first of May if I remember correctly. And it had been raining for months and months. No one went outside unless they had to for the wind would bite at you as it came in from the sea. Bored to death, I would watch the sky change from gray to black with only a hint of reds and oranges as the sun would set each evening on a drenched village. Mother would fret over her simmering stew, as father would drink his whiskey and laugh about the tide swallowing us all. We all felt stir-crazy with being locked indoors for an absurdly long winter and every few nights the neighbors would come over for dinner or we would go over there. The men talking about all the fishing they were getting out of, and the women complaining about having the men underfoot in our small cottages.

I believe it was the Thomas's that were over that night, the whole family of grandfather, husband and wife and small child. A little girl I think her name was Thelma. Anyway, what I remember most was the silence. One gets used to the arhythmical pounding of the rain on shingled rooftops and when it stopped we all noticed. The drunken pattering around the small room ceased and in a moment, all of us were out in the street looking at the silent sky. A sky that had tried it's best to beat our eardrums out with loud claps of thunder and howling winds, constant flashes of lighting hitting the tall rocks and the deep waters pouring rain down and splashing sea spray up. All of that had halted and no one spoke as they ran outside.

Now the village of Cape Rock rang with silence as everyone ran outside to the still wet streets and first looked at the gutters overfilled with water and debris. Then all as one, they rubbed their eyes hard to gaze upward at the sun burning through the quickly thinning clouds. Although it had not even made it all the way through the thick clouds that covered us, the sun seemed so bright to me. It brought out the deep blues and browns and soggy greens that had previously seemed to be only varying shades of gray in the damp lighting of the constant storms. I took my mother's hand and she patted my head as she dropped a rainlet of tear from her eye.

It started quietly at first and only the old people recognized the song that carried down through the streets. A high keening wailing song that none could understand but all could feel. A strange rhythm that simultaneously chilled and warmed the blood of all who listened. I felt my heart stir to meet the strange pulse that carried down to me through the high clouds and looked to the others around me. All stood still with ears cocked to the highest crags that seemed to be the source of the noise, many swaying gently to the strange call. The sensation it awoke was warm and inviting to the body with tones of a strange life within the tired flesh of the village dwellers. But it also had an uncomfortable and alien feel that frightened me.

As the sun began to set, the sky lit up with a rainbow of colors. The streets lit up just the same in a mirrored reflection of the reds and oranges of the clouds. As the sky faded and the world turned darker once more, the song grew louder as if on cue. And with it came a strange wind. The intertwining voices rang out sweet and terrible and clear, stirring up a stronger wind that cleared the skies. Impossible soprano highs trilled and rang over chanting altos. It we had known how to dance, we probably would have, but the mothers of all the town held tight to their precious children who squirmed about as the wind danced for them.

Slowly it picked up just as the music had. The wind swirled about the houses and spun atop the worn steeple and weather vanes of the church and townhouse. In great slow circles the air ran and danced in. Getting smaller and smaller as it neared the earth. Binding a spell that transfixed all of us. Forcing us to stand mesmerized and at the mercy to what came our way. The wind formed delicious patterns, lifting water, and leaves from the gutters in dancing waterspouts that swayed and pirouetted down the streets. Picking up miscellaneous objects as it went, such as random trinkets, loose change, wallets, and purses. Not that these things were just lying around, but under some compulsion, most of us had brought out into the clearing streets some of our most prized possessions. I tried to cry out as my favorite doll was torn gently from my hand by the swirling waterspouts but no sound came out of my throat to interrupt the song of the Banshees.

As the sun set and our valuables were carried merrily away, a new verse was added to the symphony. So much like the roaring thunder in the skies a rolling pounding beat assaulted our senses. The sound of the constant beating of many horse hooves literally shook the air and the earth beneath our toes. The women fell to their knees in silent supplication while the men shook and wiped the beads of sweat from their brows. Yet still none of the towns people talked to each other for they had heard the stories of the old ones and some had an idea of what was coming.

On and on the maddening pounding ensued into the full darkness of night. And although we began to quiver in the cold, not a step was made to the inviting hearths and warm beds inside. The sounds of the horses beating the earth made my heart lurch to hopelessly catch up to the indefinite beats, while the blood in my veins and the nerves under my skin reeled about to respond to the cacophonous chorus.

Who knows how long it went on? Minutes? Hours? Time was irrelevant, however just as I thought I would collapse under the strain of the stimulus forced upon me, just as the beating of the horse hooves had escalated to engulf all sound but the screaming women, chanting and howling and screeching in time... A resounding cry rang out like a high-pitched gong. Over the thunder of the horses and the primal melody of the Banshees, over the pounding of the sea and the howling of the strange spiraling wind, all heard the cry.

And all responded with silence.

The waterspouts created by the insane wind died out and dropped the few objects it had not borne away to some unknown destination. The thundering horses stopped their stomping with nary a whinny. And the Banshees were silenced like a bad memory.

A few of the towns' people, my mother amongst them, tried to take this opportunity to retreat into their safe cottages. She turned and pulled me along but just as we reached the threshold of the warm door, the spell was renewed. Like the pause between one movement and the next in a great and complex orchestra; just as the silence engulfed the air for an eternal moment and some were certain that the terrible hooves would pass them by. A horse whinnied like a war cry had been called, they fell upon the town like a pack of hungry wolves on a heard of helpless sheep.

A pack of wild women rode ruthlessly upon the bare backs of monstrous horses with hot smoky breath. Some of them were so beautiful and free it would break a man's heart just to gaze into her mysterious eyes. Some so old and horrid that to gaze upon her wrinkled face and matted hair would leave one cold and cursed. Together they rode in loose fitting clothes that could hardly have protected against the bitter cold.

Their horses were the largest I have ever seen. Some had colorful curly manes and tails. Their broad backs carried bulging saddlebags while the Banshees sat only on thick blankets. The heat from the horses' breaths steamed in the cold air and the sweat on their necks bubbled like sea foam. Lanterns hung in the air on the tops of poles fastened to their necks with a harness, so that they jutted into the sky bouncing to the songs evil beats. But what I remember most about the horses is the plaintive look in their eyes. They looked at us with fear and longing. They shook their massive heads at us or perhaps at their masters but obeyed their unspoken commands readily.

The young and beautiful ones leapt off their ghastly steeds and danced through the swirling wind and amongst the surly and quiet population of Cape Rock. And while they started their lovely cadences again, sighing and crying out explications to great unknown forces, the old crones leaned over their beasts and flashed their gnarled teeth as they sang a twisted lagging harmony. The likes of which I cannot attempt to fully describe although for decades the horrid sounds have haunted my memories and dreams. Slowly now the horses stamped their hooves at the edge of the circle, as it was the women's turn to dance.

A few of the young and beautiful ones carried longed soft ropes made of human hair. And while they danced they tied up the wrists of all the men and women. I tried to protest vainly as they wrapped my mother's wrists in the thick rope, but the skinny Banshee woman giggled madly and bat at my feeble hands. With one deft motion my mother was bound in their line and she was moving on to my father who looked at the woman with a blank stare of longing. She kissed his cheek with wet lips that smacked horribly then pranced away to her next victim. Meanwhile the head of the rope was being pulled by one of the oldest crones amongst them. She cackled wildly briefly interrupting her chanting as she slowly and patiently led the way out of our sacred village.

None of the adults protested to being herded up. While most of us children were almost totally ignored. It seemed they only wanted those who had reached maturity for my older cousin Bern who was only twelve or thirteen was pulled into their line while Annette his younger sister and I were left to the cold streets. As I ran at the women they only brushed me off with gentle but firm shoves that landed me a few times on my rump in the gutter. One of those times when I tried to pull and tear away at the strong soft rope, it's knots so tight about the wrists of the helpless men and women. As I pulled and gnashed at it with my teeth a pair of freezing cold hands pulled me up by the armpits and the woman with blazing hair and eyes walked me out of their circle and into the nearest doorway. All the while she sang with a piercing vibrating wail that hurt my ears.

Without notice, the line moved down the street and up towards the great cliffs looming over our village. The crones held the ends of the ropes from the tops of their steed's backs while others rode up and down the single file column pacing the speed of their new charges. It seemed to me that they moved with slowly to accommodate the many feet they led; still I had to run to catch up with them.

With the aid of the bobbing lights hanging from above the horses, I ran up and down the line searching vainly for my parents while staying out of the way of the insistent women. They led the party over the crest of the steep crags using a seldom worn trail that switched back and forth to climb the rocks. Once to the summit, they continued even farther on down a lesser incline to a large clearing.

Previously there was only a large field over here, filled with rocks and stubborn weeds whose thick roots held the soil to the rocks and the rocks to the land. I know because I had often gone exploring with my cousins on the occasional days when the rain did not beat down upon our heads. Now the field was cleared. The large boulders hauled off and the thick weeds and rocks pounded into a level circle by the methodical dance of many large horses.

The old crones led the way and lit the bonfires. A huge one in the center of the circle that was centered around an enormous and ancient tree. They didn't even bother cutting it up for they just piled the kindling of the weeds and their thick roots at its base and set it ablaze. Four other fires were lit on the edge of the circle at each of the cardinal directions. Each blazed with a terribly strange light; the one to the east burned a smoky sky gray at the top and yellow at the bottom, the fire to the south with an intense and hot red flame, the fire to the west and towards the ocean burned in greens and blues, while the fire to the north burned with flames of green. The central tree burned the hottest with an almost white flame. Above us the full moon burnt away the clouds and rare stars dotted the sky.

I watched in horror from the top of the hill as the fires were lit and bade to burn their unnatural colors. Meanwhile the people were brought into the circle standing between the women who stoked the inner fire, and the great horses who stomped their feet and danced slowly at first in a circle just inside the outer fires. The bindings were taken from the people and the baggage from the horses by three of the loveliest women. The true dance was starting and the people began to uncomfortably move their feet in search of the maddeningly changing patterns. A hard task for a people who had never learned to dance before.

Still as they were setting the circles up for the dances, a stealthy woman grabbed me from behind and threw me up into a cage on wheels pulled by two horses. Inside were several of the other children who clutched at each other in terror. The cage was bounced around the hill picking up other children as it went till by the time it got to the outer circle it was quite full. She led the horses to pull us on top of a pile of boulders outside of the northeast corner of the circle, outside of their horrid circle but a captive audience to it all. The horses were unhitched to join the rest of their kind and a group of the women came about us to sing a plaintive melody. I stopped up my ears with torn rags from my clothes and cupped my hands over them tightly. The women did not seem to mind for they did not stop me from ignoring their lullaby that put the other children to sleep. When most of us were lying about each other in a deeply induced dream-state, they left although I looked and saw one other boy named Michael holding his ears shut and looking about wildly with me. I reached out to him and he pulled me to him in a tight embrace as we looked on.

The dance picked up as the last of the women joined in, intermingling with the innocent men and women of the village. The Banshees stripped of the clothing of the men and women and forced them to dance, spinning about the slow ones and chanting horrible rhymes into their ears. Words that I could blessedly not understand although even through the muffles of my earplugs, my body and feet yearned to join and dance in their circle.

Gusts of wind blew at my back as even the wind came out to join the dance. It came in huge gusts that broke up when it hit my back and split into spiraling eddies that swirled about the magical fires in great spirals that lifted into the sky. The fires grew larger although no material fuel was added that I could see and the dancing circles grew tighter.

From my vantage point atop the pile of boulders I could see into their circle of devilish delight. The young Banshees pounced upon the naked and defenseless men, riding them like unbroken beasts and stealing their seed. Meanwhile the hags paired up the remaining men with random women from the village, forcing them to remain upright and continue the dance as they copulated. The women held tight and screamed in ecstasy as the men lurched in and out to the beats of the pounding hooves. Although neither one of us knew exactly what we were doing; Michael and I pulled off our clothes and joined each other in the dance. Awkwardly I climbed on top of him as he leaned back against the cage bars. A fit of pleasure grabbed me and took hold as he entered my virgin flesh. The crones continued their gurgled chanting at a louder level, driving the dancers on. I saw several of the men fall over in climax as I looked over Michael's shoulder. The crones pulled them up and placed some elixir of sorts on their heads and penis then applied the same to the forehead and genitalia of the women including their own. Then they found new partners for the men and women while the dance went on and on. My own partner soon collapsed like the other men and slumped down to the floor of our wooden cage that rattled with our movement and the wind around us. I wouldn't let him rest however for the pleasure and passion that grabbed at me was intoxicating. I let him stay on the floor and even though we had none of their magic potion, I pulled him into me and urged him to rock to the passionate symphony that gripped those in the circle of fire.

Endlessly they went on, those supernatural women who sang out such strange utterances. Michael pulled out first his own handmade earplugs then my own and although we tried to keep up to their orgies our immature bodies could not sustain the heat of passion that eventually overtook us. Exhausted we held each other and looked on.

The great fires still burned and we could see the wind dancing circles around them. And although I could not see it, the wind seemed to dance smaller spiraling circles around each couple as they clung to each other for dear life while the crones tied their bodies together with their ropes of horse and human hair. Finally, when they began to collapse out of their exhausted climaxes the crones let them lie there. From my vantage point the last couple standing was one of the lovely Banshees and our neighbor Tom. He barely moved although she bucked wildly on top of him chanting the names of her sacred and secret gods. About them lie the prone figures of exhausted villagers and Banshees. The horses slowed their prancing to slow and steady hoof beats until finally poor Tom collapsed under the untamable woman. The music stopped and she stood over him in silence panting heavily. Not even the wind moved and the only sound was the crackling of the fires.

One of the old crones walked up to her carrying a large unlit torch, which she handed to the woman. With a start, she took it as the old woman nodded. She looked about as if seeing the exhausted party for the first time and then angrily stepping over them all, she lit the torch off the central fire that blazed white-hot. A single horse stamped its feet in slow time and the crone took the torch and shoved the woman to the ground. Then she straddled her sitting on the younger Banshee's stomach and with strong arms she held both feet together and burned their bottoms. The crone burned them for a long time before the woman finally let out a piercing scream and threw the crone off her. I saw then the writhed feet of the old lady before she rose again to her feet to hand the torch over to the wild girl. I think now that that was perhaps a rite of passage for the Banshees between mother and crone for none of the other Banshee's feet were burned although the one with the new burnings went to all the villagers and burned their feet while the younger Banshees held them still.

Terrible it was to hear their screams and we tried in vain to cover our ears with our hands since we had lost our earplugs. As each person was committed to this cruel act of torture, another horse joined in to stamp its feet. The rhythm this time was slower as the Banshees keened softly and the crones chanted smooth words as they held down and burned another set of feet and another's. As they neared the end of the circle back to where they had started, a great fear rose in me that they would come over and burn our feet next. After all we had danced and fucked with them. But no, the circle would not be broken for two bright-eyed children and as they closed the circle once again, the Banshees returned to the inner circle with the villagers in the center and the horses just inside the ring of fire.

The Banshees blew into great conch shells and the horses changed direction and started their prancing dancing beats in the opposite direction they had been going all night. A staggering syncopated rhythm was taken up and the women on the inner circle slowly changed their smooth euphony to a string of curses they spit forth. The men and women on the ground writhed in agony and some even spoke and pleaded for mercy.

From the large bags that were set around the inner fire, the crones pulled out large bottles of thick black-green liquid. They uncorked the thick bottles and poured some of the liquid on the rocks around the central bonfire, thus releasing a stench of rotten sea. The crones shouted cries to the gods of the seas above the songs and deftly poured the viscous liquid over the screaming people. Their human moans and cries were replaced by the sounds of grinding rocks in the sea's tide. As their vocal chords turned upon themselves, so did their bodies and slowly and painfully they were changed to gruesome writhing masses of undistinguished shape. It seemed that some of the couples that had been tied together became as one writhing gurgling mass, two entities becoming one.

The memory of that cacophony that ensued overwhelms me even today as my people tried to scream through their broken throats. The horses began to moan as best as horses can to their syncopated beats and the Banshees cackled maniacally about their horrid chanting that sounded more like a taunting to the creatures at their feet. "Change!" They cried, "Show me your true forms you ugly beasts!" Their chanting grew like thunder and I felt its message in the very veins of my body. Fortunately, I hadn't been doused with that horrible concoction of theirs that seemed to make the change possible.

Through the spaces of the horses I saw them struggle to find new forms. Their burnt feet fusing together and their toes becoming fins. Their skin growing thick and tough and their arms fusing to their sides at odd angles. Michael and I held each other and cried for our people. Even through all the terrible noise and the wind and the fires, the other children around us still slept. Through the spaces between the horses that danced in endless circles, I saw the transformations take place. The worst part, I saw my father. I know it was him for his quiet features and green eyes. Those eyes finally caught hold of mine with such a look! Oh, the gods in hell were not merciful I knew that as fact now. Also, I knew why the horses had such a look in their eyes for they had lived through this before.

As dim rays of light began to show over the horizon from the east, the wind blew straight over us from the depths of the vast land into the mysterious and unfathomable reaches of the sea. The sounds of the transformed died down and the witches rolled about in gay laughter, breaking open flasks of liquors, which they shared in the last hour of night. They even shared with the horses and their new creatures, pouring the stuff down their new mouths and placing the spirits in deep bowls for their steeds. Their spell had worked it seemed and their mighty fires began to burn low in the strong eastern-born-wind. Their chanting ceased and turned to conversations in a strange tongue filled with intermittent laughter.

All chatter ceased at the sharp command of the oldest and ugliest crones. She spoke as she looked towards the east and the brightening sky, then boldly walked out of the circle towards the west and towards the large overlooking rocks. Quickly the women tied the creatures to the steeds, lifting them to their broad backs with surprising strength. Once secured, the horses carried their loads after the old crone who had vanished out of my sight to climb the rocks. I heard no sound but the clomping of the heavy hooves as they retreated from the circle and the dying fires.

The landing on the tops of the rocks was almost out of sight and we could only see the back of the crowd as they gathered. After a long pause of silence, the old crone yelled a few short curses and immediately I heard a loud splash of something large thrown into the sea. Then again, the cry of curses and the loud splash. Over and over again the terrible sounds of my people thrown into the sea.

The horses retreated down the hill and to the outskirts of the magical circle. A few of them came over to us in our small portable cage and I reached out my arm to pet them. They shied away at first with worried glances to the rocky hilltop. As the sounds of the splashing grew more frequent one finally came over to me. I pet its large nose and looked into its sad eyes. "Let me out." I pleaded. The large steed looked over his shoulder once again then bit off a knot of rope that held the door shut.

As the door swung open the other horses pricked their ears in attention but did not move except for the ones coming down the hillside. Their big eyes of blue and green and brown nodding to us in approval. I stepped down out of the cage and off the boulders, Michael followed me hastily with big tears streaming down his face and snot running down to hit the ground. "Father!!! NOOO!!!" He cried and raced to the hilltops. I heard the cackling of the old crone then one last splash.

I ran after him but he beat me to the top. As I approached he looked at me in a panic and gestured out to the ocean. As the sun crested the horizon, all I saw were the torsos of the Banshees riding away with the west blowing wind on the backs of giant sea creatures. Their barely discernable forms like nothing I had ever seen in the sea before. As I joined Michael to the top I could see they were far away. "We've got to join them." He said to me while tugging at my hand.

"No." I said. "We've got to tell our story."

He looked out to the sea and back at my face. Then he kissed me on my cheek and said goodbye before jumping off the tall rock. I looked over the edge and cried out as I saw him hit the water swimming with all his might. In a few moments, he somehow caught up to one of the sea creatures and the Banshee on its back took him to sit in front of her. There I stood, all alone, the last of my kind and the only witness to the demise of a beautiful people. I watched the backs of the Banshees disappear in the spray of the sea. They rode proudly and resolutely into the unknown with a steady patience of those on the road in a long journey. Where they planned to go and what horrors they subjected their new charges with I can only guess at. I only wish I had seen what types of creations they had transformed the little fishing town of Cape Rock into. On the other hand, perhaps it is better left unknown.

As I sat there on the crest of the rock shivering in the bright morning sun, a large red-haired mare walked up to me and very gently nudged my shoulder. I turned to look at her and after she let me pet her, she looked intently at the cage at the edge of the circle. The smaller children were just waking up and I walked down there with her and helped the children up, waking up the few who still slept soundly. Together we walked back to our village on the other side of the rocks only to find it burned up. It was as you see it today only some of the fires were still smoldering. I walked through the deserted and burnt up street in a daze while the children behind me cried and wailed for their absent parents. The horses followed us and stood back with loving patience. I found the storehouse unburned with stores of dried fish and fruits. Then I recruited some of the other children to help me pack up supplies in nets and bags. All the while the horses looked on with approval.

When we were finished packing the bags I went over to the horses who let us tie the heavy baggage to their backs. Noticing the just a little too human quality about them, like the way they fidgeted and nuzzled and touched each other and the children. Their whinnies sounded strange and muffled as if their voice boxes had been distorted and the soft hair of the manes on many of them grew in curly waves like I had never seen on a horse before. Feeling comforted by their presence, we loaded what was not destroyed that would be helpful on our journeys then mounted their broad backs sitting only on the heavy blankets that were already tied about their chests and soaked with sweat.

As the sun rose to mid-day, and for once not even a single cloud rose in the blue, blue sky, we rode out to the east. Against the strong wind that blew in our faces and warmed us with a strange hope. Homeless and guide-less, the horses and our small pack of about twenty children rode out into a harsh world to fend for ourselves in the great depression. Many of the younger children found homes to go to while the rest of us wandered about with our wild horses that looked after us as we looked after them. Although I had never menstruated before, I became pregnant from that magical night and gave birth to a remarkable little girl with sharp sea green eyes and untamable dark hair that always grew straight out of her head. I named her Madea and raised her the best I could as a young roaming gypsy. It was a hard life, but we seemed to manage all right with the help of kind strangers.

Although it was almost fifty years ago, the memory still clings vibrant to my soul as if it were only yesterday. I feel a weight lifting now as I finish my story for now I have told it and perhaps can cast out at last into the sea on my strong and small clipper in search of the terrible Banshees who took my parents. For I'm swept into the wind of a strange dream that calls to me. Beyond the known lands and perhaps beyond the sea there lies a place where I belong with the

Banshees if they will have me. You see, my dreams have been plagued by the visions of a strange nirvana, the same dream that the Banshees sang about as they rode off under the cloudless sky so many years ago.

The Wings of Night

I tried on some wings tonight and found a
way to fly away. Just where I got them I
cannot say for even clowns and fools have
secrets.

The sky shook as it took me into its realm and the
clouds poured down their heavy rain to try and
shake me down. But I just laughed and shook my
dreads, then flew through chaos all over town.

The bats they flew right by my side
while the strong wind blew and the
ravens cried.

I flew to the place of haunted hills, to see the
ghosts and goblins play.
They showed me their secrets of frightening thrills, and showed me to
see in a secret way.

And when the night came upon the hour
of the dead. The filthy bones of dead
man's souls crawled out from the graves
and to the night arose.
Into the darkness, I was thusly led.

Under droplets of rain we danced around

I laughed and cried while they made no sound. Yet they brought out their jewels and magical tools.
With their help my spell was cast and bound.

As we completed our rite such a magical sight cast down
on our circle the light of the full moon breaking up the
chill and gloom.

And in the dark and chilly black, unearthly howls sent the dead men back. Into the graves from which they rest with untold secrets upon their chest.

From there I gathered up my tools and strange unearthly magic jewels. Then I stretched my wings and took a light and flew into the silent night.

I cackled then as the rain poured round. For nothing now could keep me down. Till at the first dim rays of dawn, I landed nimbly upon my lawn.
Then crawled in bed with a smile for I knew
That my work was done for my will to come thru.

Illustration By John Arnold and AAA

The Gods Down There
Autumn-01

 Ah, welcome at last to my world of darkness and beauty. I'm so glad you followed me here to see my exotic secrets. Here blood red and the deepest of purple roses grow and flourish with thick thorny stems and leaves so tough they feel like thin leather. But you must go deep to find them, I've only seen a few in the deepest and blackest of sewers and underground caves. Tonight, I will take you down there and together we will discover new secrets.

 And if only you could see in the dark you would know of the beautiful world in which I speak. For the darkness harbors exotic and dangerous creatures who shun the revealing rays of light. I know, sweet one, that you too are a creature of the dark and mysterious. I can tell by the sly, deep look in your eyes and your silent lips that utter not a single word and nary a sound. Some would think it a great tragedy to be mute, but I find it alluring and compelling. All the thoughts that must go racing through your minds but with no way to share them. Oh, I admire your courage to live in such a cruel world as this, which is why I want to show you a different way and a different place where silence such as yours reigns supreme. Truly such as you have never before dreamed of the silent and beautiful places I will take you.

 Won't you follow me down these long stairways to my secret places under the city? Fear not for I shall hold tight to your hand while I reveal the secrets of the brackish ponds and deep catacomb tunnels, you shall be under my protection. Or perhaps under my spell. I do hope you don't mind my ceaseless prattle but I have this great urge to tell you all I know and see. You're such a good listener and I know my secrets are safe with you.

 Here is the first gate at the secret entrance from the too darkpark. A simple and plain looking sewage drain. But don't you find it funny that it sits atop a small hill behind this bush like so? I did, the first time

I saw it, and my insatiable curiosity drew me down into its depths for exploration. I didn't get far but I got far enough to know that this is a sacred doorway into an ancient and diverse world far different than our own. Tonight, however we shall go as far as we dare, for I have all the supplies we shall need for such a journey. Some food and water, a few candles and a flashlight, some extra socks, and a thick blanket we can share if we get tired and need to rest. I do hope your jacket will keep you warm enough, it can get cold down there. Are you ready? I will light the first candle and once our eyes adjust to the dark it should be all we need. Come silent one, take my hand.

What is it that first drew me down to this place? Ah, perhaps it was the intense solitude that I sought after. For only the foolish, the hideous and the shunned dare to venture to these dark and long-forgotten places. And down here, we are family when none was to be had in the upper lands under the sun. Perhaps I shall introduce you to some of my friends if we run into them, for they do like to wander the halls just as much as I. That is of course if you think you can handle the sight of them. For some of them have certain deformities and illnesses that have driven them down to these depths.

Oh, breathe in deeply, my dear. Do you smell that rich soil that surrounds us? This tunnel is just high enough to walk in although I do have to stoop a bit. When we get deeper, the tunnels will get higher; it is only this first part in which we have to bend over slightly. Don't worry too much that you will trip over or crash into anything, for the path is relatively clear as if it gets cleaned out on a regular basis by some unknown entity. I also love that sweet smell of mild decay that wafts through the air down here. We are under the old cemetery after all. Some of its crypts are so old that the writing has worn off. I've heard rumors that this used to be a sacred burial ground for the natives for hundreds of years before we came here. Now that I've been underneath the crypts and shallow graves, I'm not surprised that the dead are chosen to guard this dark, dark secret. Apparently, colonists just took down the ancient markers and built their crypts right above the ancient graves of generation upon generation of Native Americans and who knows what else. For I have a strong feeling that human hands did not build these tunnels alone.

Well you'll see what I mean when we get further along.

Ah here it is, the gate that leads under the cemetery. I know it's too dark to see well but you can reach out to feel it. It's beautiful! A true piece of hidden art (like so many things down here). Its ancient cast-iron is delicately engraved with demons merrily leading new charges into the depths of hell. Feel here, that is the proud demon Danubis eagerly hefting the unwilling down the long stairs. The stairs are steep and according to this, they once ran with blood and were littered up and down with the bodies of the sick and plagued. My favorites are the roses that delicately line the boarders. So, detailed they are and some of them so soft I could almost pluck one to put behind your ear. Stand still now...there.

Now the key, it should still be under this stone...ah yes, I feel it. I remember the first time I had found it. The stone seemed to almost call out to me to lift it. Underneath it was a skeleton key made of solid gold, so heavy. I picked it up and tried it in the luck just like this. *CLACK CLICK CLICK WOOSH SCREEEECCCHH!!!*

I feel you shaking but don't be alarmed by the sounds. Under here everything sounds louder as the ears strain to detect what the eyes cannot see. Just let me return the key to its place and we will be on our way. I could take it with us, but I feel that others should be allowed down here too, if they dare to come.

Don't try to turn back now dear. I know it smells unearthly down there but you must look beyond the darkness and the strange if you are to find the beauty that lies there. I was scared the first time I came down here too. Ha ha ha! In fact, after I opened the door, it made such a ruckus as it swung open with just the slightest push that I ran up the stairs as if the demons of hell were ripping at my heels! Only to realize when I was under the bright light of day that I still held the key and had to go down to replace it. I'd also left the gate open and it took all the wits I could muster to go back and close it. Come along, I'll shut it behind us as we go down so as to not let the dark ones escape.

Anyway, when I went to sleep that night in my apartment, from out of the depths of dream the key beckoned to me, with a hollow gong like tone, I followed down these very steps in my dream to the place where the immortals dwell. They seemed to be ancient gatekeepers sleeping restlessly under the pounding humming city. Marking time and the growth of man they sit down there watching and waiting while keeping safe their many dark secrets. Waiting and watching with silent shallow breaths, their bodies lie almost still while their minds and spirits wander. Watching and waiting and finally calling to a select few of whom to teach.

You will soon see, feel, hear, and understand them with me. For I remember in that dark, powerful dream they spoke to me and told me to find a mute and bring him down with me. A silent powerful one and a brave and fearless one like yourself.

Mind yourself on these stairs now, they are narrow and some of the decayed. Hold my shoulders whilst I lead, for you don't want to touch the wall too much. Thick slug-like creatures live on them feeding off the moss and moisture that comes through the earth. But if they are given the chance they will not hesitate to latch onto your flesh, oh your soft delicate flesh they would love! I had one attack me once and that was enough to urge me to learn steadily the way without disturbing the native creatures.

Just ahead is a landing and a hallway where lie the catacombs of the city's ancestors. Ah, here it is, level ground for a bit. And look'! Have your eyes adjusted to the darkness? Can you see how the walls are glowing faintly? In just a bit I will be able to blow out our candle for as we go further down in this enchanted place, a luminescence often prevails in places like this that have never before seen the light of day. The farther down we go the brighter it will get as if this most holy of all places is lit from the core of the mother earth herself with her strong energies.

Perhaps that's from all the energy that gathers here. It all collects with this heavy presence as the energy of the earth below and the city above filter down and coalesce here. Oh, look at this puddle of water! It just shines as it gathers the spare energy into itself. Such a warm, eerie feeling as it gathers in my own body… Don't fight it now, let it flow with you too.

Just about all of these tombs are sealed up. The bodies inside are left to rest and decay in peace. See how their names shine with that luminescent glow in some strange and archaic language. It is proof that long before the white men came, before the Native Americans even there were ancient ones who lived here. Perhaps they found many of the tunnels and improved upon them or maybe they made them to protect from the harsh elements of a changing world long ago. To hide from the hideous beasts that lurked upon the surface in ancient days. How far these tunnels and caverns reach I can only guess at for there are some especially dark places where a cold wind howls so that even I dare go no further. Tonight, we shall travel till we find the answers to the riddles that call to me. I hear clearly the summons of the ancient Gods that urge us ever deeper. We may take a little time getting there. I figure as I'm showing you this place, I may as well take you through some of my favorite spots.

Like these tombs for instance. Look here at this one that's cracked open! If I peer inside with my candle I can barely discern the outline of a skeleton for even their bones glow with that phosphoresce that permeates everything down here. And look this door's been ripped right off! Why these bones positively radiate light! They must be so old yet were somehow petrified or calcified so they won't decay anymore. It looks different than we do though, it's eye sockets for instance. They are much wider as if made for larger eyes while the nasal passage is only two small slits in the bone. His few teeth are sharp and small in a narrow jaw.

Could this be the missing link? One of our great ancestors? You can touch his forehead if you like and sense his great age. He comes from a time when the surface was too cold and sparse so mankind lived down here in the catacombs. The tunnels bustling with life and activity. They even farmed plants and livestock down here, for their pictographs show strange beasts walking through the tunnels with them. Please don't try to take the bones with you though, I'm superstitious.

Now look, all that's left of that Dark Age is in these secret halls. These long lines of vaults stretching from floor to ceiling in places even lining the floors we walk upon. If you look down, you can see what's left of the engravings on the floor. I could only wish to be placed along the ranks of ancient mystics, priests, and laymen when I die. Oh, how I wish I could read and understand the words written so thickly down here that glow with their own devilish light. What strange rites could they reveal?

Oh, do you feel that my dear? The slow pumping vibration? Although I've tried in vain to find its source I know what that is. For every city has a soul and a spirit that beats with life. That *hum hum thump hum hum hum thump* is the city's heart. Perhaps someday if I please the ancient ones enough they will take me to see the enormous pumping flesh of the city's heart. Perhaps this time they will be happy with you...

Alas there is so much to see down here, we shouldn't linger too long we still have a long way to go. At the end of the catacomb corridor is another gate. Well go that way.

Gasp! Do you see that pale snake poking out from the hallway? Even it glitters with its own magical light. And its sheer size! Its head as big as my foot, only filled with poisonous teeth and blind eyes. That thick body could probably digest half a human in one sitting! Oh, I hope you stay put lovely creature for I won't disturb you too much if you don't harm us!

Fortunately, I'm protected by a beautiful talisman that the Gods gave me. See this amazing stone carving! One side has the face of an ancient God with a large head and bulbous eyes and jeweled crown atop his head. The other side had glyphs in their ancient language. And coming out from it are all these strange arrows. I got it down here a while ago that's why it glows with its own light too. They whispered the talisman's hidden location to me in a dream and the next day I came down here and found it. That's also when I received the call to find you and bring you down here as my beautiful witness and charge. The Gods are calling to us and so long as I wear this and you stay by me we'll be safe down here. Safer than anywhere above ground at any rate, with all those crazy people blowing up buildings and crashing their cars and planes and shooting each other…

What a sanctuary this secret land is. I'm so in love with it all! That, and I feel sheltered, protected, and accepted. Where others perceive me crazy in the lands above, I am suddenly deemed welcome and sane down below for I can understand the great ones as they speak directly to my soul through energy and emotion. I'm not the only one that feels this way; there are many mortals that live down here. Hidden in shadows, some of them are probably watching us right now. No need to fret my dear, most of them are harmless unless you're an unwelcome guest. But believe me, you will be made most welcome down here in this sacred world. Walk softly around the snake, see now, it barley reacts to us for I am only a shadow to it by the God's protection. They are like the secret ones that live here, they know our strengths and would rather have us work for them than fight them. At least that's how it was when I met the men at the springs.

We will go there to see the immortals who watch the world with their astral minds.

What do they eat you ask? Oh, different things I suppose, moss and mushrooms that grow down here, rats, sewage, plus some things I've seen them eat that's made my stomach churn. We do sometimes make food runs for them raiding garbage pails or surplus stations. They don't seem to need much and there are many ways to survive down here. Like I said before, we provide acceptance to the shunned and function like a family or community.

Hey you asked that by telepathy, didn't you? You have more talent that I had thought. Oh, the Gods will take great pleasure in you, I'm sure of it now! They're looking for a few select individuals to train too... Well I'll let them explain it all when we get there. I'm a little foggy on the details myself right now, I just know that it's important enough for them to wake from their eternal struggles and call to us. They told me that if I did a little recruiting for them, they would make me immortal like they are. You'll have to see it all to know and understand but perhaps they will give that option to you too!

Here is another gate and it leads down another long flight of stairs and some of the lower living quarters of the ancestors. I come and go by a back way, which is how I took you here. Few of the under-dwellers know about this entrance. That's why they're not in these parts. Perhaps we will run into some of them below though.

See how this gate glows too? It's made from a strange metal. Black Jack says it's made of meteor metal from when the meteors crashed to the earth thousands of years ago, to make the lakes and oceans. I tried asking the Gods if that was true but they wouldn't answer me. They can be stubborn like that sometimes; they don't like to be bothered with trivial questions keep that in mind.

This gate has pictures on it too only they are simpler than the first one, but I think it's a map of the catacombs. Here's a great sea beast on the bottom you see it? Like a giant squid or something that these people are tending to. Look close, it's almost as if some of them are jumping into its mouth to feed it... Then the stairs that climb up and up through storerooms and living chambers where people are working. The images are dim from age but you can make them out. This and that one look like workshops for tradesmen and that one looks like a bathhouse. I tried to go this way once to the bathhouse but the way was sealed up from a collapsed ceiling, closing off the entrance to mortals and perhaps trapping the mortals inside.

Damn, it's locked! I wonder if there's a key hidden round here like at the other door. Let's see I'll start looking round, you see if you can jimmy the handle.

Click click Clack! RRUUUURRrr*!!!*

Hey did you do that? You did! Why I never guessed that you could pick ancient locks too! And you just nod and smile in your silent way. Damn you're beautiful, have I ever told you that before? NO? Well you are, and even down here you have eyes that I could just melt into. Those Gods are really going to love us you know. And we can sell them on your hidden talents like lock picking and telepathic communication.

It looks dark down there. I'm almost getting second thoughts about going through with all this. Something feels different this time. But we've already gone this far and you did just open the gate… I'll just light another candle to help us. Maybe it will scare away some of the nasties I know are lurking down there. I'm not defenseless though. I've got my switchblade here. It's pretty simple but plenty sharp… as long as we don't run into a sewer gator that wants us for dinner we'll be ok. Come take my hand I'll lead the way.

… … … … tick tap tick tap tic tic tic tic… tick tap tap tap tap tick tick tick tap tap tap…
… …… … tic tic tap tap
tap…

That sound is either one of two things, and I hope it's just the water dripping off the ceiling…

Tic tick tick tick tap tap tic…

Gee, it's sure getting cold down here…

Tick tap tap tap

I wonder how far down we are. It feels really deep and my ears need to pop like when you climb a high mountain only the pressure on them is greater here, not weaker.

Tic tic tick tick tick tap tap tttt
Crunch!! Rrrmmmm

Oh, watch these steps right here, they're a little disintegrated. You know, I bet if you went far enough down here you'd find the earth's core...

Tic tick tap tap tick...

Are you scared? I am a little bit but I think I'm more amazed by all of this. It's so magical down here we're so fortunate to see it all, I mean no one knows about this place, not even the explorers. And then there's simple old me to just come down here and stumble upon it. No I was drawn to this place really by this intense feeling in my stomach and chest that told me to come down here. Then the last time I came down here I found this amulet and the Gods spoke to me. Really! I heard them. They told me to bring a silent witness and they would show me their secrets of immortality.

Tick tok took schuullpp!!!
"Uuuggg uuuggg!"
Gasp! Oh no! It's one of those giant slugs! Get off him! Get off him AARRGG!!
Pooh Pooh tic schuulp pooh thud
Oh, Gods are you ok? Look at you, you're bleeding!
Rrriippp rriiippp ppp!

Here we go, we'll use this scrap of my skirt to bandage your arm, it'll be ok now. Didn't I warn you not to touch the walls? Well I think it's dead, I stabbed it a few times then it just fell off you. That one was big, wasn't it? Almost a foot and half... You're still bleeding but I bet the Gods will fix it for you. Come on let's hurry down, I can feel we're getting closer. And don't touch the walls!

Tic tick tick tap tap tap tic tic tic...

    I guess that really is what's making that noise. It sounds like there's lots of them down here. Careful here hold my arm with your good hand. I have really good balance and won't need to touch those slug-infested walls.

Tic tic tic tic tap tap tap Tick tick tap tap...

    There's so many of them they're even blocking out the phosphoresce glow in the walls. I wonder if that's what they normally feed off. Careful where you step they may even be on the floor too.

Tic tic tic tic tap tap tap sssqqquuuiiissh pooh pop!!!

    Ohh Yuck! I'm glad I'm wearing big combat boots, I just stepped in one.

Tick tick tap tap tit ti ti ti ti tap tap tap ti tic tic tap...

    Oh finally! Look there's light ahead and the stairs end! I think we're there! Yah!! It looks so bright ahead.
    Gasp! Shangri la! Look at this have you ever seen anything so amazing? Glowing towers of stalagmites answer the crystal encrusted stalactites hanging from a ceiling so far above that I can barely see where it ends. So enormous! They must have been here before even the ancient ones themselves! Look how these quartz crystals have grown out of the formations. Like great candelabras they glow each

with its own individual light! My! All the colors they make, don't you see the miniature rainbows everywhere? Each one different like this one! It's a rainbow all right but the tones are all purplish, same with the ones around it. Where are they coming from, I wonder? Ah, look at this cluster of amethysts. It's so brilliant down here, lit form within with its own light. And these dark ones, aren't they smoky quartz? The original black light I bet. And look at its rainbows not definite colors, more like it's made from shadow colors. It goes from black-red to dirty-orange and yellow, a smog green and dusky blue, but that purple indigo! They look almost like solid shadows sitting out from the wall. There's more crystal clusters there too; greens and red and blues... All of them seem to be in some sort of order that I can't quite make out...

Wow, this place is strong with power! I feel like my whole body is being charged off these crystals. So massive and perfect some of them are. I don't think I can ever tell anyone about this place, or at least where it is for they would surely come down here and destroy it, I just know it. I am almost tempted to take one of the crystals though...

No, no, no, I don't think I should, this world is too sacred and I shouldn't loot from this magical power spot... I just can't get over how big it is and how perfectly intentional yet natural it all seems.
And the cavern goes on even further! Let's go.

Gasp! Stop! Do you see those men lying there? They must be the Gods who tend this place. They look so old just lying about like sea lions in rays of the hot sun. Come on, let's go talk to them. You ahh, just stay quiet and I'll do the talking ok?

It's not as bright in here but I hear the sound of water trickling. Those massive stalactites hang almost to the floor! And look at...

"Who goes there?"
Hello! AHHhhh!!
"Who's there?"

Oh, it just my reflection that's all. Um hello? My names Autumn and this is _____ my silent companion. We come seeking the Gods down here.

"Come here child so I can see you." Oh yes, I'm sorry... Hello.

"A woman! My it's been a long time since I've seen one of those. It's been a long while since I've seen any outsiders in fact, I had figured the rest of the world was probably deserted and dead by now. You shouldn't have made so much noise though, things like that can cause quite a bit of damage down here."

I'm so sorry sir. It was that mirror, something in my reflection just startled me.

"Mmmm, what was it you saw?

I, I, I'm not really sure now actually.

"You should look again before you enter this sanctuary."

Oh, ok...Gasp! My reflection it's changing! No, no, no, it's not true!

"Of course, it is. That is the mirror of truth. It shows the viewer the true form of their souls. So, tell me, what do you see?"

I see a creature like only those I've seen in my dreams. It's like my real image is being superimposed with a dragon creature. It has large wings and a scaly face with large gray eyes and a pointed chin and...

"Your wings what color are they?"

Um, they're kind of translucent and dark. Black and red and purple, deep blue at the tips of them.

"Ah, a powerful one you are! And on your forehead, do you see a symbol child?"

It's ah, kind of flickering but I can make out a star.

"With how many points?"

One, two, three, four, five, six, seven; seven points. The star of the west gate. I had a dream once that I was leading souls across the great abyss of death, is that what I really am?

"A dragon guide for the newly dead, yes the prophecy is coming true at last! Tell me girl, how did you find this place?"

The Gods called me down here and told me where to find the entrance and the key. Are you one of the Gods?

"For fear of lying to such a beautiful power I must answer honestly. We are a clan of immortals and these springs you see here are our source of everlasting life. As to the Gods that you seek, I had heard rumors long ago of the Gods residing amongst these rocks but never found them myself. I am simply a gatekeeper here, I was once called Janus... Now your friend what do you see there when he stands before the mirror?"

I see a bright angelic child looking about with wonder.

"Yes, yes, yes, the new spirit and the old guide. You said the Gods called you down here eh?"

Yes, in my dreams they led me to this talisman and through the tunnels down here.

"Very nice! Quite the plans they must have for you. But first let me help you two get more comfortable down here. Come follow me... This is our haven the Gods made for us to keep. We've been down here so long that I'm afraid we've lost track of time and the upper lands. You may look around if you like."

Ok. These pools, all of them are different and these old men! Why they look like sea lions lying about in rags. Come let's talk to some of them.

Hello sir, I've come to ask for your immortal wisdom...hello? Are, are you awake? He feels cold but I can see his chest moving ever so slightly. Maybe he's hibernating or something, I'll try another one.

This man looks like he's sleeping too. But look how long his beard is! It reaches out from his still body in a long-tangled mess that's twice his length.

"Uuhhh!"

Huh! Oh, he is awake! Hello sir, how are you?"

"Uuhhh, gurgle gurgle"

"What?"

"Gurgle gurgle, glub glub."

Um perhaps they are like you and cannot talk. Can you speak telepathically with him? No, well it was worth a try. Hey look there's a man over there sipping from one of the pools. He is at least alert, see how he looks at us where the others seem to notice us not at all? Perhaps he can talk to us.

Hello, hello?

"Uummmm bladda bladda bota umm uummmm"

Oh! Let go of me, don't drag me in there!

Twak!

Gasp!

"Arrada, arrada flatee infiniante! Don't trouble yourselves with them too much child. Their minds are not in their bodies for they oversee much greater places than this. Sometimes I do have to discipline them with my cane to make them stay on task. For you see although they look to be frail old men, their minds are directing the movements of the universe like in a great orchestra!
Very important work!"

Oh! Well I hope I didn't disturb him too much. But he looked at me in such a strange way!

"Yes, we will have to hope that your actions don't shake the planes he is forming and training in his mind. Such things can have dire consequences even if they are not immediately seen. Now, come here closer and let me get a good look into your eyes, both of you! Ahh! I can see that you speak the truth about your message. And your heart is brave though your mind is foolish. I also see that you have the talent to manipulate other to your will.
You must remember to use that gift wisely and not to abuse it. I see that your friend here did not come down here of their own free will but felt compelled to come at your bidding. Do not fear silent one. You may find it very inviting down here. Your bright mind can be put to very good use while you need never speak if you so wish.
Ah, your injured. Was it the slugs?" Yes.

"I will mend you, follow me."

Thank you, Janus. Your realm is breath taking by the way. These colored pools, they look so intriguing.

"Each has its own purpose in the balance of things. They're concentrated liquids feed springs all about the Earth. Each one with a different yet essential purpose. This red one here, it will heal your flesh, give me your arm…"

Amazing! The flesh is binding before my eyes!

"Yes, down here Magic is very strong and real. May I offer you drought of our finest waters?"

"I won't be trapped down here if I try them, will I?" "That would depend on how much you decided to drink. Come over to our blue pool, it is the purest."

What a lovely goblet you've handed me. Thank you may I toast to life?

"To life."

Ah! Amazing.

"Careful just a sip or two will be enough."

Thanks. "And to your friend." Here you go.

Hey slow down! Don't drink it all! Stop! It's empty.

"We must all make our own decisions. Now listen carefully while I direct you to your destination. Go on down this way to that hall over there, you will see it when you come around the corner and recognize it as they right passage by the Dark Rose Bush near the entrance. There you will find a pool you should bathe in to cleanse the upper world from you skin. After that take the centermost tunnel to the Camber of Crystals! The passage is long and steep and very dark in places, do you have a light?" Only a few small candles sir.

"Take this then. It is a glow rock, part of what makes everything glow down here. Only be sure you drop it before you get to the surface if you ever get back there. You be careful now, you have my blessings, and the Gods give you unspoiled riches!"

Oh, thank you Janus. I think you've been a great help for I'm sure we would have gotten very lost if it weren't for you! Would you like some food from the world above?

"Oh, you have some!"

Yes, be careful eating it, you may have a sensitive condition to this but here is some bread, and some apples that grew under the light of the sun.

"Yes, do give here and take care now! I see you wear an amulet of protection from the Gods but still be wary. The way is more treacherous than your foolish mind thinks and some creatures disregard the wards with wanton malice. Like the prowler for instance. He's got an excellent sense of smell and probably a near empty stomach. He won't come in the sacred chambers, but if he sees ya' then you better hope he's too weak to move fast. Yeah, I'd say that running would be your only chance against him. Good luck Fools, may the Gods have mercy when you reach them so that you may live to see the sun again."

Good bye then! My he left in a hurry! With no good bye and he's such a sad look in his bright eyes. Well I guess we can rest when we reach the bathing pool and don't worry I still have some more food for us. Are you ready to continue! Good let's go.

Look! There's the rosebush! I think, I mean what else could it be? I've just never seen black roses before, so cryptic! To touch them gives me the chills, and its smell, like sweet dirt and musky death. And in a place where so many things have a light of their own, this rosebush takes in the light instead of giving it. The thick black-green leaves and thorns shining so darkly with stolen light!
Don't touch but look at those thorns! They're so thick and just dripping with some viscous liquid, poisonous to be sure. Ah, to pluck even a single rose and place it behind the ear would surely mean the sweet kiss of death. And here we are at the doorway that Janus spoke of. It's edges crudely shaved from the solid bedrock. And the walls are now lit with intermittent crystals that catch the light from my rock and reflect it a thousand-fold! Perhaps they've grown out of the rock, or the rocks have grown around them, but look at their solid bases. And each one larger and more pristine than the one before. Oh, this is such

as amazing path, with the regular crystal torches and the smooth floor. I can feel it going down and down though. We must be miles below the surface by now.

Huh! It's slick in some places, tread carefully...

Those old men were kind of creepy don't you think? Could you imagine how bored they must get just sitting down here forever? That old man said their minds were occupied somewhere else, I wonder exactly what he meant by that... Their bodies looked pretty messed up though, like withered prunes. I wish I had asked him how old he was. He probably would have said something crazy like 1000 years!

Really, you think he was even older than that? Hum. Yes, perhaps but I can't imagine what one would do with all that time. I think it would drive me insane, but I guess that is why I am young and they are old.

Oh look, you see that light ahead? It looks like it's coming from water!

Ah, this is the pool he told us to bathe in. It does look so inviting and that waterfall! It's so tall like it comes from high above us. Down to this secret place where hardly any dare to walk. They are both so iridescent that the water looks like a prism all the way through it! Well if we are to bathe then let's do it.
Come on, take off your clothes!
SPLASH!

Oohhh! This water is hot! Almost too hot, but if I swim over to the waterfall it's better, come over here, I'll scrub you down. My this feels incredible! I've never been in such sparkling water! I do feel totally cleansed by it, almost tingly. Ah, I fear I can't stay in here long this heat is almost overwhelming. Come, let's eat while we dry, I've got some good food and I'm sure you're as hungry as I am.

Ok, I've got some bread, energy bars and water. I gave all my apples to the old man. Well let's drink this water. The energy bars we should save for the hike out of here because we'll need them later. The bread and apples we can eat now. Umm, I was hungry you know…

Hiss tick tick tick tick…

'What was that? The prowler? He sounds scary, I hope we don't really run into it. Even though there's light of a sort down here, you still can't see very well. The shadows and nooks and crannies are so big. Anything could be hiding in them really. Did I see something move?
Ti ti ti ti ti tick tick…sss…

There it was again! Ohh, I can't tell what direction it came from. Everything kinda echoes down here. Even our footsteps seem loud. Ohh, let's put our clothes back on I don't want to be caught unawares. SSSSssss…ssss…tititi tick tick tick…
Come on let's keep going, hold my hand!
Look at all these entrances! Which one do we go down now? And they all have rose bushes in front of them!   SSSss Ti
ti tick tick Sssss ssss…
Ahhh, that noise is closer here. I guess I better choose quickly, it sounds like something is coming after us! But it sounds like it's coming from that way. We'll go this way. I think this is the center…
SSSSsssssss…..
Wow, this tunnel is brighter than the others. So many glowing rocks sticking out from the walls randomly… And the floor is smoother here, like it's been polished smooth at one time. I wonder if the Gods made this place for themselves to live in down here…
Look! It's the end of the tunnel, I think I picked the right door after all. Do you see that rainbow light? It must be another room of crystals. Wait don't go in yet, let's take a peek first.
Holy shit! Those crystals are bigger than we are! with the different colors, red, orange, yellow, green, blue, purple… It looks safe, but my

what a heavy force of energy this room holds. Like the energies are so thick I could bite the air! It's almost hard to walk in but come... Ohhh, my! That big one in the middle. It's so big and clear and twice my size! Yet it looks perfect! The points on the top and its clear flawless center that turns opaque in the bottom. I feel a pull to come and touch it, yet I'm afraid to enter the circle.

 SSSSSS ti ti ti ti ti ti tic tap tap tap ssssssSSS!

Huh! It's that noise again. Like it's following us! AHH, I didn't even notice those! Giant black quartz sitting so strong in the corners, looks like there's four of them in this room, one for each direction, maybe they keep the magnetic poles of the earth in balance.

"Ti ti ti ti ti ti ti sssssss, ssssss, ssssss what kind of treeessspasser are yeee! SSSSS"

AAHHHHH The Prowler! Stay back I carry a talisman from the Gods and any who harm we while I wear it will be damned by them! "Hhee hee hhheeesssssss sss ss, I'm already dammnned by the Godsssessss. Thisss placcce iss mmy pprrisson whicch I musst guard from trssspasseress ike you!"

No no no! I'm not a trespasser! I was called down here by the Gods in the center of the Earth! I come seeking their message and have brought my silent witness that they asked for in my dreams! *"SSSS ti ti ti tick tack! Yeessss, it issss time finnnally."*

AAHhh stay back! Don't eat us, I might not look strong but I'll put up a fight if you try anything! See this knife! It's sharp and I'll cut you up with it!

"SS sss sss sss you will neeed a biggger knife than that to ffffight meee!!! SSSS!!"

Creature of the dark, I am under the summons of the Gods from the middle of the Earth! I sense we are almost at our destination! Do not interfere with our holy quest unless you intend to help! For I will not stop until the Gods show me their promise to make me one of them.

SSSS I aammm the great God Danubis of the Dark! Forever condemmmend to guiard these pilllarrrs of light that maintttain the balance of the eearth. For alll that thesss Goddssesss are, I am efverything they aarrree not! Nooowww ssss telll me. SSSSsss Do you really wwissh to join the ranks of them in this iimmmoorrttal chamber?"

What is this place anyway?

"Theesssee arrreee the ttime keeepppers of thiss world. For ages nooowww they ave been ffrrozen in theese cryyyssstallllssss as they muusst remain stilll to hold the ffabrik of rreallity together. Noowww they only dream while I guard. For what they dream becomes fact. Ssss you children arrreee only ddrreeamssssss." If we are dreams, then what are you?

"SSSssss what do you sseee?"

I see a nightmare with sharp teeth and a forked tongue framed by a scarred mouth and black skin. Your claws are sharp and long and hit the ground when you walk, making them click. Your thick skin looks like ancient hard leather that still sucks the light out of the air about you. You look so black in this bright place with a menacing aura but I see your eyes too which are filled with secret knowledge and a glimmer of hope at my presence. You are the gatekeeper than you must also be the guide. Then you would know what the Gods called us down here for?

"SSsssss Yesss! Takke ooff your tallisssman and III willl shhow you."

No, I dare not take it off lest you try to trick me.

"Yesssss, very well thhough II wiill nnot harm you. I hhaave losst my appettite for humanss looong ago. Iiff your tallissssman is true than it issss the keeyy to the lllock. Ttrry itt! Ti ti ti tick tick tak"

Where is the lock?

"SSSS lllook iinn the flooor!"

Ah I see it. Yes, it's shaped like my talisman kinda. Here is the glyph with the arrows coming out of it, but it is engraved with more glyphs that I cannot read. What do they say?

"It ssayyas that the oone witthh the key sshhall hhave the power to create a newww wworld oout off theeir oown. The keeeyy! Tick tick tick. Does it fit?"

Yeah it looks like it, but I don't know if I should turn it. What if it changes everything in our world?

"Then you'vvve only to dream of the nneew one and sssince 'twas you turned the key it shallll beee aasss yoou sssss dreammed!"

I just don't think I can do it. Is this what the Gods wanted me for?"

"They did call you down here! SSSS lisss that why theeyy wanted hhiiiim? Find out and ttuurn the keeeyy!"

I, I, I don't know. Think about this first with me, does it feel right? Yes? Ok, do it then and be done with it.

Clack clack wwiirrrr!!!

"Aaahhh yesss. It isss sstarting. I have waited fooor sssoooo llooonng. come here young human! Teelll me, what dooo yooouu ssseee in hheerre?"

I see an old man frozen inside the quartz. he wears an almost sheer robe and he clings to a large tomb to his chest, the binding of which is chained to his wrist. The quartz that holds him is clear and almost flawless save for a band of cloudiness above his head near the termination.

"Yeessss! Do yoouu know wwhooo that issss?"

It's God!"

"He iiss a God yeeesss, Tthee God no. Thhiss isss desstiny and the boook he carries hold the sstory of thhe unnivversse from sstart to present. So long as he sstayss in thiss crysstall, hummanns may rettain their free will and write their oown chapters upon hiss ghgreat boook. If desstiny iss unloocked however he wiiill write the chapters and lives of allll mortals in an eefffort to speeed hiss time of exxxistence. Now ssilnet one. Walk around destiny thrree times then knock near hiss chestt three timeesss."

No! Not him! Me, they told me that I could join their immortal ranks if only I brought a silent witness!

KNOCK! "Sstaayy ffoool!" KNOCK!!

But!

KNOCK!!!

"Your immmortallity sshall come in a diffferent form for yyoouu arre to doccumment theessse events to sspparkk the new belief if the old Goddssessss. Yoour name willl be remembered alwayyss while yoourr friend'ss ssoul here wiiilll lllive on always in this realm, sssillent and draming. SSSoooo much hassss desstiny told me."

His eyes they opened! We're not going to set them free are we? His crystal is lit up! Ohh what have I done?

"Yoou my dear have sstarted ssomenthing much biggger than yoursself that cannnot be sstopped. But yyouu wiiilll see wwat is too come ssoonn eenough. Now letss move on, theerreee isss a lot of woork to do. SSSstart in the east whencce creation hass come and tell me what you ssee in the red crysstal!"

I see the outline of a man who has no solid form, yet his light shines bright almost like the sun. His hands are holding a beautiful branch of ivy and his blue hair is spread about as if in a strange wind. The crystal he stands in is red and flawless save for the stream of clouds above his head and at his feet. The crystal is darkest near the bottom but it lightens with the light from the man as it reaches the top in a band of cloudiness.

"Ssilent one, walk aarround him tthree ttimes and knock three ttimes. Tthis is Aairrre founderrr of ccrreeeation, movement and aacction."

KNOCK!

KNOCK!! Whoo whoooo!!

KNOCK!!! Whooo whooo aaahhhhhhhh!!

That wind! Where is it coming from? His eyes are open now too and the wind is alive! Oh, Gods, what have we started here?

"Thaaatt wasss gooodd. Noow the orange one. Wwhat do you ssee?"

I'm afraid now. I can't finish this! You intend to destroy our world all just to end your bondage!

"Quite the ooppossite ladyyy, though yyoourr fear iss jusst. One should be unssetttled at the makking of aaaa nneeww wworld for thiss is sooo much bigger than yoou and III and hhhiiimmm. Yyoouu cannnot sstop what you hhavee sstarted,. If you were to leeaave bbeffore we're done, there would be oonly a bbblaack hollle where thisss new Earth sshould have bbeeen and thiss blaacck hoole wiill do nother but conssume everything around it. Nooww tell me what you ssee in the orange crystal!"

I see a beautiful woman of dark skin and thick long black hair. She is large and very powerful and her belly is full with a child. Her gown is made of fine fur and her feet are bare. In one hand, she holds a large root and in the other seeds. Her crystal is bright orange at the top getting darker and deeper towards the bottom like rich clay soil. She also has a white stream of energy running from her head to the top of the crystal.

"This is Survival and Growth, the mother off thhe true Eevve. The cchhildrensshe holdsss arree to be the first of many on a new world where they wiilll learn to surrvive through love and hate. Ssilent one, walke arrround her thhreee times and knock three titimes near her sstomacch!" KNOCK!

KNOCK!!

KNOCK!!!

Her eyes are open now and she smiles at me as she drops the seeds!

"Go nowww to the ssouth. Tell mee what you see in the yellow srysstal."

I see a man whose clothes are frozen in a silent flame. Even his head is covered with hair of flame. His skin is dark black but unmarred. In his hand, he holds a staff. Again, his crystal casing is flawless though the color varies widely from deep yellow at the bottom to lighter at the top where his band of white energy reaches out of his head.

" *This isss Fire, and like the sun of creaation, hiss sseearing ttouch ccleaarss the wayay for neeww life and pushed oolld life into eevveeloution. Ssillent one pleassseeee.*" KNOCK!

KNOCK!!

KNOCK!!!

Yes, his eyes are open now too and his garments of fire are moving! Oohh, suddenly it's very hot in here as the reflections of flame lick at the walls.

"*Go noww to the Green crysstal.*"

In the green crystal, the floor is thick with deep green plants that grow up the legs and become the dress of the woman inside. Only her breasts and face are exposed through the foliage. In her right hand, she holds a chalice and in the other a bow knocked with an arrow.

"Thiss isss Love, she is paasssionate ssteaddy and peerrssisstnet through at timesss her touch caan bee ruuthless for heer call is evveer pressent in aall creaatures. Ssssilen oone, knock att herr hheart for that is where she is ffelt." KNOCK!

KNOCK!!

KNOCK!!!

Her eyes are open now and they too are deep green and yes, I feel her pulling at my own heart with her powerful love and ruthless nature. Her light only adds to the heat in here now.

"Go nnoow to the blue crystal in the wesst."

This blue crystal is such a deep blue that the color barley fades as it reaches the top, yet still I see the white band stretching from the top to the head of the man inside. His pale skin and beard give him a wise and old appearance. He wears a crown of seashells and fine jewels. In his righ thand is a large conch-shell and in his left, is a trident. He is clothed in what seems to be shark-skin or some other sea creature's pelt.

"Thiiss isss Water. He giivess life to ssubstance whhiille he washess hiiss children in poolls of cool dreams, SSsss without him, there iss helll. Ssilent one, walk about him annnd knock!" KNOCK!

KNOCK!!

KNOCK!!!

His eyes are open and he is lifting his head to me! Now the floor is leaking water into the room! Oh no! We can't be flooded out!

"Tell him to ssstop!"

Yes, right. Water, stop your current until we tell you to release it. For the time is not now and the place is not here. When the time is right our spell shall culminate, and whisk you away to release your floods... Yeah, his feet are holding the water out but it is still slowly coming in. We must hurry so we don't drown. "Go then too the indigo crysstal ssss."

This crystal is very beautiful. Well they all are but this one is... The colors change in it with a sort of geometric pattern and the white band of light through it spirals onto the head of the woman inside. She has pale skin and long dark hair that hangs down in tight braids. She is clothed in a simple yet elegant dress that matches her crystal and she holds a book in her left hand and a large quill pen in her right.

"This is Thought, the divvidder of ssimple liffe formss and compleess ones who hafve the ability to create. Sssilent one, when you knock, knock at her head sss." KNOCK!

KNOCK!!

KNOCK!!!

Her eyes are open now and she is opening her book to begin writing.

"Before she writes moreesssss, sshee willl recite the magical ritees that will open the tree gate for the new wworld ssss! Goo now to the violet crystal!"

This violet crystal seems filled with more substance than the others, like it is made with very complex layers and more than just one color although violet is the predominate one. The white band from the man's head is very thick. The man inside looks ageless like most of them do but he is also very round and happy looking although there are sores on his hands and face. He wears a coat of bright weave that looks like forests and mountains and rivers all over it. His pants are blue like water. In his right hand, he holds a marble sphere and in his left a crooked wand.

"Thiss is Earth, aand the ssores you ssee on him are the effeect of mankinds abussee. We will heal those woundds beefooree wee coopy hiim for our neew planet. Sssilent one walk around him tthhreee times and knock thhree times, sss ssss sssssss." KNOCK!

KNOCK!!

KNOCK!!!

His eyes are open now and yes, the sores are getting smaller. RRUUMMMMMBBBLLLLEEEEEEE!!!

HUH! What was that?"

"Aaahhh that wass our plaacce moving. Sssoon we will strassport to oouter sspacce wwhere thiss nneww world will form. Wwee don't have mmush time left quickly nowww. we are almost done. Before wwe goo to the lasst one in the circle, we musst oppen the dark crysstallss tooo! This is the firsst. Tell me child what do you sseee?"

This crystal is so black that I can barely see into it. There is a red tint to the whole thing and as I look closer, the form of a cloaked figure becomes apparent in the center. It is wearing a thick cloak of blood red and is holding a bottle in one and a scythe in the other. There isn't a white band from her head though, instead it is light red that goes from the top of her head to the top of the crystal. That is Death, isn't it?

"Yess, with liffee allwways theree must be Death. She is perhaps the wissest ooff them alll for sshee must decide whheen each ccreature's task sss arree done and then bring them tooo her.

Ssiilent one, walkk around her threee time and kknock each time.

Wait! Must we bring her to this new place?

"Without likfe therree isss nothing, withoouut death therree iss no change, without change threeer iss no ggrowwth, wwwiithough groowwth theres iss no liiffe. You sseee without death there iss only nothing! Yes, it is necccesssarry." KNOCK!

KNOCK!!

KNOCK!!!

Her eyes are open now and she is pulling back her hood! Oohh, she is beautiful as she smiles! Please lady death, avert your touch from me for a long time, I want to see and do everything before I die!

"Enough of thattt now. I don't tthhink sshee hhears you anyhow. Come alloong to the nexxtt dark crysstall."

This crystal has a bluish tint to the blackness, and inside is a large man dressed in heavy armor. In one hand, he holds a fierce morning star, and in the other is a huge hammer. He wears a horned helmet and the ray from his head is blue to the top of the crystal.

"This is Destruction, Death's brother. He wieldsss the morning star of wwaar and the hammmeer of changin forcesss. Mmany ttimess over, he will destro tthhe old ssoo new young life mmaay grow. Ssillent one, please... KNOCK!

KNOCK!!

KNOCK!!!

His eyes are open now and I feel great fear in response to his power. He is also lifting his hammer!

"Wwheen the ttime isss right hee willl ccreeate the new field of creation by destroying the vvooid tha tliiees therre now. come now to the next darrk crysstall."

This dark crystal is yellowish in color and inside is a frail looking woman dressed in rags. I one hand she holds herself up with a crooked cane, and in the other is a begging bowl. Although her feet are bare and her hair is thin, the yellow line from the top of her head to the top of the flawless crystal is thick and solid looking.

"Thiss iss Destitution. Ssshhe lives in tthhe form of poverty and dissseassse. Without her, life would noot worrk ssooo hard to change an dimprove to get riid of her. Ssillent one please knoat aatt her feet."
KNOCK!
KNOCK!!
KNCOK!!!
Hey eyes are open now and she quivers as she stands there.
"Very well veerry well. On to the lasst daarrk crysstall."
This dark crystal is a strange greenish black and the man inside is wearing modern type dress clothes. He has a long graybeard that falls past his feet and he holds a stone tablet in one hand and a pocket watch in the other. There is a green band of energy from his head to the top of the green-black crystal. This is time is it not? "Yesss, Faather ttime. Hhee almost forrgot about me tilll hee sent you hheeere. At last it is time! Ssilent one you know what to do! SSSSsss!!!" KNOCK!
KNOCK!!
KNOCK!!!
DOONNNGGG!!!!!
RRRJUUUMMMMBBLLLLEEE!!!!
What's happening?
"The firsst bell hass tolled. The begginning of creation is almost finnisshed! Oone last crysstal to go. The eighth in the inner cccircle."
This crystal is so bright it's hard to look at. The color is like none I have ever seen before, so brilliant, and strong! So strange, I've always dreamed that someday I could see beyond our color spectrum, it's like a reddish purple yet so strange and bright to my eyes. Inside I see only a seed with a band of white energy flowing to the top of the crystal. What is it?
DDDOOONNNNGG!!!
"This is Ultra Violet and the spirit sseeed of the neew wwoorld. It iss to be filled with neew ccreeatures ssince it was created by a woman and a mann, ssoomeday it will be filled with a nneww rrace of mann.

Ppeerhaps yyoouu wiill iincarnate therree someday too aandd bee aamong the ffirsst of the women to live there.   Nnooww it iss time ffor the placing of the ssoouull.   Eveery thingg in the universe hhass a soul including the planets and suns.   Noww iss yourrr ttiimme Silent One. Three lasst knocks and theerree isss nno looking back." KNOCK!

KNOCK!!

KNO- DDOOONNNNGGG!!!!

RRUUUMMMBBBLLLEEE!!!

Where did he go? Aahhhh! Everything's shaking!

"Look inside again!"

I see an embryo, is that him?

"Yesss, thhee neeww sould is an old one!   Ha ha ha ha ha ha SSSSSS ha.   It will be upon himm to dreamm annd create eeddeenn again sssss."

DDOOONNNGGG!!!

No no no! What have I done? You're going to destroy Earth, now aren't you?

"No no, III won't do that.   Yoouu humannss have alreaddy sstarrteed!   Ha ha ha. . .   You sshhouulld go nooww iff you wwant to live to wrritte about thiss.   Not that any will belive youu anyway. But first tell me wwhoo III am."   You...

You're Chaos aren't you!

"Yesss!   All that theesse Gods are not is what III am!"

RRUUUMMMMBBBBLLLLLEEEEE!!!!

"Here, take this small crystal that led you to this place for yourssself aand a rosse ffrroom the doooorway.   You have only a ffeww mommmennts to esscappe frreeoom eetternity!!! HA HA ha ha ha ha ha ssssssssss.   GGGOOOO NOW!!!

Oh! Goodbye then, send my love to the new planet for me! Don't forget love!

"Take a rrroosse to remmember love!"

Ah yes, of course love is everywhere! Yes, I will take this one the-oww! Shit those are big fucking thorns! There I got it, and now I'm bleeding!

DDDDOOOONNNNGGG!!!

"Hurrry morttal! there's no time left!"

Ok, here's the door and my crystal is almost throbbing with light so it hurts to hold it. I'll hang onto it though, it may be all I have left now.

DDDOOOONNNNNGGG!!!!

RRRRUUUUUMMMMMBBBBLLLLLLEEEEE!!!!!

AAAAAAHHHHHHHH!!!!

SSSPPLLLAASSHH!!!

GASP! FUCK! This water's cold! Hh, hh, hhhhhh, hh I think the floor must have fallen through or they've left or something. I wonder if they're going to take those poor old men with them?
They said they weren't Gods but I wonder… … …

Well, at least my crystal is still glowing, I can kind of see around here. Just looks like a tunnel filled with water. Well I think the flow is going this way so I should just start swimming with it…
RRRRUUUMMMBBBLLLLEEE!!!!

BBBOOOOMMMMM

BBBOOOOM BBOOOOOOMMMMMM!!!!!!

RRRUUUMMMMBBBLLLLEEEEE!!!

FUCK, Gods, please don't let this ceiling fall on me!

AHH, look! I see light up ahead, like an opening to this cave! Same way the water's flowing too!

Wrr wrrr, wwrrr Aaahhhh!!!

"SSSCCCRREEAAAMMM!!!"

"HELP ME! Somebody help me!"

"Look, there's people in the water!"

"Try to hang on to this we'll get you out!"

What's happened? An earthquake? Oh, they're throwing me a rope.

"Good, stay there, we'll get you out!"
"Here, grab my hand!"
"Yes! That's it! Steady!"
"I got you girl. You made it!"
"Come over here lady, why don't you sit down for a bit ok?"
Ummm, I'm ok. I think so.
"Let me find you a blanket or coat to wrap around you. Sit tight ok?"
"Here's a blanket, give this to her.
"Great! Here you are lady."
Thank you. What happened?
"This flood sure is crazy, isn't it? There's been an earthquake and it's like the ground just opened and started spewing out water. I could have sworn you came out of the hole down there too! How'd you get down there?" Huh?
Under the ground! Did you fall in a ditch or something in the flood?"
I don, I don't know. "Hey what's that you got there?" Um, a crystal and a rose.
"I've never seen a black rose before. I'm surprised that you managed to hang onto it and swim and that it didn't fall apart on ya'. Hey Jess! come over here! My name's Hal by the way. I helped pull you out of the water. What's yours?"
Oh, look I've got to go home and um, check on my pets. "No, you need to stay here till we make sure you're ok!" No, I'm ok. I just need to leave now bye.
"Hey! Going so soon? I didn't even get your name! Well I think you should keep the blanket at least."
I'm sorry, I've got to go. Thanks for the help! "Sure, no problem. What no thanks even?" Thank you, the Gods bless you too.

A dream, only a dream. Could that have been real? I just don't know. But look at this rose. It's tough like leather and deep, deep red, almost black, but it's real! Death, her color was this red, does that mean she granted my request?

All around me the chaos and confusion of destruction. The dark man wielding his glowing morning-star, clearing the path for something new to take the place of the old and stagnant. There's always change, life and death are balanced.

Something new, a new world, caused this earthquake, a world that started from a piece of ours, a world I helped create.

The Garden of the Star Lilies

"There is a way to step from this world" I heard
the voices whisper as I walked beneath; The
imposing shadows of pine and alder. I turned
around at these words but found only laughing
squirrels and chirping birds.
I walked up a lava stream bed and found an altar
Hidden behind a fallen tree and surrounded by white flowers, three.

So delicate and soft were the silken petals
Shaped like star tips, soft as sacred flesh
The light scent of pollen transfixed me on my knees.
I sat in the sacred space and held a crystal to my face
And with the breath of God, divine light shone through the trees I
closed my eyes as fragrant winds passed through my hair and my
spirit lifted through the lofty air.

I awoke in a garden that was surely a tribute to Venus. Moon Dragons
stood at the gate and bowed as I passed Yet there I did hesitate to
look around at the heavenly bodies to be found.
Far in the sky sat the Earth, the Moon and Mercury too.
I lost my step and breath and did nearly swoon Yet
Venus' Fairies came to my side with tinkling bells
led me inside.

There I walked past filigree silver gates, into a
garden made for the goddess with dreams, love
and sacred bliss.
A cool breeze drifted through my hair
Intoxicating pollens filled the air I bowed my head to
flowers divine my head was filled with delectable high.

In a giddy trance, I collapsed to the pale soil
And stared down the earthbound stars
Little flowers shone with the light of Jupiter and Mars Delicate petals of seven whispered of fairy heaven. My eyes turned to tears and my face to blush My body swept away in an exhilarating rush.
I cried out in joy but the trees whispered "Hush…"

As I looked up from where I lay
A host of spirits advanced my way.
They carried, so carefully, gifts, for no mortal to see. But look upon them I did at last What I saw there made me gasp!
Sitting in a bowl of crystals so rare Was a terrible Demon covered in hair?

I tried in haste to retreat, but the Demon jumped to my feet. I was dragged through flowers of the moon While the stars raced and I was knit into a cocoon.
I had dozed where no mortal should nap And found myself in an awful trap One thing saved me from an awful eternity, my lover in bed gently waking up me.

Illustration By Naomie Seraphina

Dancing Nightmares

Upon the summons of a golden ticket, I board a blood-red chariot on a cold moonless night. I'm pulled through the night by a dark steaming beast gilded in silver that glitters like twinkling stars. The ground blurs beneath into light-years of cobbled stones. The streetlights flicker by at great speed, mimicking the flutter of candles burning in distant rooms. Cold wind bites through my heavy cloak and random snowflakes bite at my fingers and nose.

The fiery eyes of the dark beast light the way and a hissing roar is sounded as we approach the party. Chilled revelers hug the high stone walls and frosty gates. Their feather laden and glittery masks tremble in their eager hands as they draw lots for admittance. I am fortunate however, for as my chariot squeals to a jarring halt before the gate, tall men in black top hats take my hand and guide me past staring eyes, flashing bulbs, and raucous laughter.

Gargoyles hiss and growl in great fun, nipping at the sharp heels of the ladies and swiping at the men's motley caps. Yet it was the brutes in monkey suits who decided which of the revelers would have the privilege to enter. I brandished my golden ticket with a flourish that was met by a deep bow by an ape in a red suit. I glided upon a thick red carpet gilded with gold spiral weaves. The gates were shining gold that flashed momentarily when I crossed the threshold.

A dazzling array of laughter, lights, music, and smells assaulted the senses. The whole scene was so overwhelming I could scarcely see to the end of the richly populated hall. The chandeliers dripping with crystals created refracted rainbow confetti that fell about in sparkling profusion. The smells of ginger, wilted roses, sweat and wine mingled to invite my soul to intoxication. The masqueraders around me bow and nod with generous recognition as I take in their motley forms.

*"There were arabesque figures with unsuited limbs and appointments. There were delirious fancies such as the madman

fashions. There were much of the beautiful, much of the wanton, much of the bizarre, something of the terrible and not a little of that which might have excited disgust. A multitude of dreams dancing with blind passions. *And these – the dreams- writhed in and about taking hue from the* sprawling decorous halls, *and causing the wild music of the orchestra to seem as the echo of their steps."* All of them wore some type of mask or facial ornamentation, and through these gruesome facades stared eyes bright with malicious glee. In the high corners of the hall, jesters juggled and jigged, contorting into disquieting shapes and spinning flames at the ends of long chains.

The band was a motley crew of Seely hosts. Dressed in high fashion of riotous garb, they stood upon a tall pedestal overlooking all. Such instruments and musicians I have never seen, (nor shall I see again)! Their horns curled about their twisted bodies, taunt strings were hammered plucked with vicious nails. I think I saw you there, playing at the fiddle with wild abandon, your coat tails flying as your pounding feet struggled to keep time with the drummer. How one could play next to an angry ape is beside me, for he banged upon those drums as if he hoped to make the earth quake and the chandeliers fall upon the dance. Indeed, I did feel the heavy pulse of the bass throb through my feet. Waves of noise rose and fell in great swells and it seemed the lion trombonist lead it all proficiently with his racing melodies.

The throngs of masqued merry-makers were compelled to dance in intricate mating patterns, and as I was trying to observe the steps they took, a strong red hand gripped my elbow tight. I turned to look into the face of a red demon encrusted with jewels all about his face and brow. Large red horns protruded from a mass of dark curly hair that nearly hid the sharply pointed ears. He only said two short words to me before I was flung into the dance, his strong arms guiding my feet across smooth mosaic tiles.

"May I" He said and without waiting for an answer he took the liberty of spinning me round between laughing corpses and nimble nymphs. I squealed in protest and the Demon laughed, opening his mouth wide so I could see his sharp teeth and smell his putrid breath. I quickly lost myself in a dizzy frenzy, as we passed between sweaty masqueraders in an orgy of sacred communion to the dream and the dance. The Demon held my hands a little too tightly as he led me in rapid steps that nearly had my feet tripping off the floor! I was simultaneously engrossed and revolted by the Demon's long dark hair and strong red muscles. Yet his clothes were stained a suspicious hue of red and a smell like burning death crept off him and rubbed into my hands and cloak wherever I was touched.

Above me I could see fairies flitting about dropping mischievous glitter upon contorting cadavers. I was whisked past a long table heaped with delicacies that would only please the revolting tastes of Nightmares such as these. At that first glance, I saw a pile of squirming squids covered in thick syrup while the Demon dragged me to the bar for a drink.

The bartender was a purple eight-armed demi-deity and he smirked as he poured from several bottles at once. The Demon paid him with a couple of large coins he produced from his pocket and handed me a simple glass goblet. I tried to refuse the bubbling berry-sweet brew that was pushed into my hand but it did smell good!

Sweet ambrosia! My tongue tingled with just a little sip and already I felt an uplifting rush. I raised the glass to my lips, pausing to enjoy the sweet smell, the pure red nectar that bubbled just so...

Suddenly a tolling bell shook the entire hall with such ferocity that I dropped my glass! I gazed down at the liquid that burbled and burned at my feet. When I looked up, my attention was brought to a massive clock tower that reined at the far end of the hall. It was so gaudy and monstrous that I wondered why I had not seen it before.

All manners of revelry had paused at the mighty toll of the first bell. By the second beat, the band had stopped playing and all eyes were turned to the dark face whose two hands were positioned to the time of eleven o'clock. The roman numerals glowed as if lit from behind and those and the glowing hands stood out in sharp contrast to the black frame shaped like a great hooded man. Upon the third toll, a door opened within the clock to let out a small line of ghostly drummers.

With this strange band came a strong gust of deathly cold wind. All around me, Nightmares screamed as they were plucked from the crowd randomly and pulled into the air. Their bodies spun in a corkscrew over our heads and were swallowed by the haunted clock. The Demon who had pulled me into the dance was among those that were pulled into the air. Of him I saw no more.

The Nightmares around me ducked in fear and clutched their masks tight to their faces. I checked that my little cat mask was firmly in place and felt the smooth velvety fur upon my cheeks. My cute little ears were snuggly upon my head and if I shook my hips just right I could make my long black tail wag. My calico skirt clung close to my hips and flared at my shins with what I hoped was a becoming patchwork of brown, red, and black.

By the time the clock had struck it's eleventh toll, the air-born Nightmares had vanished and the air hung heavy with an ominous silence. The Lion trombonist tapped his music stand then blasted the first few bugle notes of a swinging jazz number. I stood on my tiptoes to look at the band and saw that you were still there playing the fiddle with new purpose in your strange mask that gave you a long-pointed nose.

Gradually the party resumed, the dancers went back to the dance and the drinkers back to the bar. I had lost my thirst for a drink and was looking around for a new dance partner or someone interesting to talk to. I saw several stunningly beautiful women in outrageous outfits whom I longed to go and talk to, yet they were surrounded by overfriendly acquaintances who were kissing their fingers and whispering behind their masks. I sighted one beautiful woman standing quietly listening in on a circle that I thought I could try to speak to. She wore big black feathers tipped in red round her neck and her mask was made of black and red sparkles. I began to make my way towards her when an old batty hag thrust her beady face into mine.

"New to the Nightmare Ball eh?" She said and the smell of decay poured forth from her rotting teeth. Her costume was trashy with bits of stinking debris sticking to the hole-filled fabric. A mask disguised her face, yet huge bat ears protruded from her head, between them she wore what was once a feather hat but the feathers were plucked bare and only the stalks remained.

"Oh, um yes. First one in fact."

"Oh, how delightful! Just keep your mask on and you'll do fine dear."

"Yes, I will. But where did they all go when the clock rang?" I asked.

"Well now, don't you worry too much about that old clock. It's just taking us off to our jobs is all. You know, we can't all be at the ball at the same time, there are millions of dreams to haunt and even on holidays we must work. Tis a pity they don't give us overtime pay it is now. But then again, being here does give me some fresh ideas. I might even get a couple of sharp owls to do a double with me. What do you think about that hooter over there?
I think he likes me!"

She was pointing to a tall owl wearing a mask that made him look like a frightened mouse. When she waved at him he turned the other way as if he didn't see us and was involved with another conversation with a large wolf.

"Well, it's worth a try, have you talked to him yet?"

"Oh, I would but I'm just so shy. My names Bertina by the way and you make such a lovely cat! What would you say to racing through some dreams together sometime? You can scare them up the trees, then I'll chase them out for you! He, he! Such fun it could be. Look here, I'll give you my dream quadrants and you come spooking around anytime you feel up for a good laugh at the expense of the little ones!"

She produced a dirty bit of cloth that she scribbled on with a crayon then stuffed into my hand. "I didn't get your name yet."

"Oh, well, I haven't given it. My names – "

"No, no, let me guess. You look like a – Selina?"

"No."

"Um, Shadow? I once had a cat friend named Shadow, tricky feline there, let me tell you. I swear he was the best hider; it would take me entire nights to find him once he decided it was time for hide and seek. Of course, if I was ever lost real good he seemed to have a knack to help me out. I sure do miss him, I wonder if he made it too the ball..."

"Well, Bertina, there are a lot of haunts here, it may be hard to find him. I'll keep my eye out though."

"Oh, would you? That would be just sweet of you Kitty. Do you mind if I pet you? You look so soft and cuddly."

"Um, actually I do." I said and did my best to extricate her wandering hands from my head while sidling away from her. Of course, each step I took backwards, she just met with one forwards.

"Oh, well let me fix your ears for you, they look a little crooked now they do." She licked her fingers and ran her grimy hand over my temple and hair, which made me cringe with revulsion. Where was that beautiful Demon when I needed him? Well, I would have to get myself out. I saw an opening in the writhing crowd and quickly darted through and once I got a safe distance away from the old Bat I joined the dance.

The dancers around me waltzed in neat organized circles, each partner caught up in their own rapture of eyes and whispers. Their steps were beyond my comprehension and besides that, I didn't have a partner. I ducked beneath upraised arms and spun around twisting bodies. My mask fell lose and, partially blinded by it. I stumbled into rich dancers and heard a woman scoff. I quickly apologized while fumbling with my mask and trying to find a clear place to stand.

"Please madam, allow me." Said a silky- smooth voice and I felt my mask lifted in place a deftly tied beneath my hair. I felt sharp cold metal against my neck which gave me the chills and when I turned, I looked at the painted face of a jester, complete with the harlequin checked pointy hat and ruffle collar. He wore red, blue, and black checkers that made his skinny limbs hard to focus upon.

"Oh, thank you." I said and bowed quickly before the handsome man. I saw his face smile beneath his checkered mask.

"You're welcome. You seem a little lost."

"Oh, I think I am. My um date disappeared a few moments ago,"

"Ah yes, the time clock. It gets the best of us it does. But no need to think upon the other realms now. It is a lovely holiday and I also am in need of a partner. You can't go around by yourself here you know, or that turning of the clock will get you for sure!"

"OH!" I said in surprise. He deftly took my hand and kissed it. His miss-matched green and blue eyes sparkling at me behind the mask. "My name is Nimble Nick."

"I am Odom Pandemonium." I replied. "Nice to meet you Nick."

"The pleasure is mine beautiful kitty. May I have this dance?"

"Certainly."

He was a splendid dancer; he led with grace and finesse that wove us between the other dancers with not a toe scraped or an elbow bumped. I was in deep admiration of his tight flexible body and silky silver hair and scarcely took my eyes off him.

"So, what matters of Nightmares do you haunt?" I finally got up the nerve to ask.

"Ah, I'm a specialist. A lock smith you see." He took his hand from my arm and waved his fingers before my face whence I saw the many keys dangling from each finger. "I know the secret passages that the Gods forgot about and can slip past most any lock they set to keep the likes of me out. Why I didn't even have a ticket for the ball tonight and here I am! Simple really when you know the language of the locks. They like to be licked just right, especially when they're tight!"

"Oh! Ha ha!" I chuckled for I was at a loss for a better reply.

"I'm a highly sought after man in some circles. Why just last week, I had a job from a group of soul smugglers to unlock the hidden secrets in an old woman's delirious mind. That was an interesting job I tell you."

"So, you're a good dream than?"

"No, I wouldn't necessarily say that. It depends on how you look at it I suppose. Or on my mood too, sometimes I open doors for the eternally running victims and give them a way into another dream. Other times, I shut the doors that naughty children leave open. But what I love to do is haunt bankers, for they are so greedy and sure their safes are impenetrable!"

This elicited a hearty laugh out of me and as I looked up I noticed that we had crossed a good portion of the floor and were nearing the head of the hall where the mighty clock hung above all. Below this sat a very fat King dressed elaborately from crown to sparkling toes. On the throne, next to him was a bone thin Queen, her gowns stark and simple yet radiant in a special way. As the dancers around us approached the end of the dance line, they paused in their dance to bow before the royal couple. Nimble Nick made no exception and he led my hand to a velvet gate where we were to bow humbly before them.

"Have you a gift?" Nick hissed into my ear.

"Um, no!" I said suddenly panic stricken.

"Then I will give them two necklaces, one from each of us." From a hidden pocket, he pulled out two jewel bedecked necklaces set in chains of bright gold. As we bowed, he placed them in the hands of an uppity porter who set them in a growing pile of jewels, antiques, and fine crafts.

I thought my eyes would pop out of my head at the sight of such a pile of booty. I was certainly thankful for my kitty mask now to hide my shocked face. The King laughed at the sudden flip that Nimble Nick performed directly after our mutual bow, and the Queen nodded her head at the both of us, her eyes lingering on me (at least I think they did). I starred at them with my mouth hanging open and Nimble Nick took my hand and yanked me back into the dance as the next pair of dancers came up from behind.

"Your new at this aren't you." He said gaily. "What gave me away?"

"Only your awkward bow and popping eyes!"

"Was it that obvious?"

"Oh, no of course not my lady. Now enough of that, tell me about your best Nightmares!"

We danced with such ease across the floor, I felt instantly calmed as if I could and should tell this handsome man my whole life story. Yet as he requested, I told him of my nightmares full of laughing demons tearing out bloody guts, chasing zombies that tried to act like my friends until they were biting into my arm, and of course the clowns. The terrible frightening clowns that haunted my cirkus shows, jumping in at all the wrong moments to steal my spotlight that I had worked so hard for…

"Really?" Said Nimble Nick. "Tell me more about these clowns!"

"Well, just the other night, I was dreaming that I was doing a real neat flaming trapeze number, I had wicks going up the chains that held my trapeze and I lit it up just as I climbed on with a giant staff. While I hung upside-down swinging my staff around, in come a troupe of clowns ready to do their classic firehouse stunt and they banged their big ladder into my legs on the trapeze and when I tried to bat them off, one of them lit up like a candle. The other clowns put him out with much ado while at the same time they were acting like they were helping me down, but really, they were hosing me off with their high-powered water guns. Once I finally got down they slammed a giant pie in my face and my beautiful act was ruined! To top it off, they pulled down my pants in front of a huge audience that was laughing uncontrollably. I ran back stage and they were teaming about, little midget clowns and they were like killing people with popcorn and cotton candy, I don't know how but... Well it sounds silly now I guess but it was a terrible dream."

"Your right that the clowns are silly, are you really afraid of them?"

"Oh no, not usually anyway, I've had several good friends who are clowns though we always seem to have unsightly partings in the end, but when they're in my nightmares, they just plow right into everything I've been working so hard on and just mess it all up."

"Ah, I see." Nimble Nick said with a sly grin. "How would you like to tie them all up and put the trick on them? I've got the best collection of locks around and could show you how to wrap them all up so tight that Houdini himself wouldn't be able to finger it open."

"Ha ha! That would be fun. Maybe I could really saw them in half once I've got them in a box."

"Why not? We could haul other dreamers into it and earn bonus hours while we're at it!"

"Oh, joyous! Sounds like a deal!"

"Shall I pick you up for a dream-date then?"

"Well, perhaps." I turned coyly and in response he ran his cold key-tipped fingers down my spine.

"I could take you to the most secret places you never thought of like the center of the Earth or the Fairy's forest glades. I've seen where the Cheshire Cat hides his calico body although it's not as nice as yours. I even know where Old Jack the Ripper hides his lethal blades! But to get to the center of a girl who lives in her own secret world, what a treat I should find within that delicate meat. Where chocolate cherries turn to red blood berries and candy veins are laid out like window panes."

I gasped in realized fear of this dreadful dreams true intent, and whilst I turned to escape a sudden tolling bell rang throughout the hall. Immediately the band stopped playing and the throng of revelers turned to look at the massive dark clock that tolled out the slow beats of midnight. A cold chill blew through the room that stank of stale death, around me many a frightening nightmare huddled in fear.

"Come back here!" Shouted Nimble Nick over the third beat of the clock for I had taken the opportunity of the distraction to slip into the silent crowd. All around me, nightmares rose into the air and spun a spiraling dance into the vortex face of the clock. Nimble Nick caught hold of my dress sleeve with his jagged key-tipped fingers and tried to pull me to him. I jerked the other way and as the clock tolled six, he was pulled into the air above me. I spun on my heels to watch with my eyes as he tumbled and turned, spiteful swears upon his lips that could be heard above the tolling six, then seven loud bells. Those around me laughed as the clock tolled nine, and at ten the vortex had swallowed him. I sighed in relief as the last of the souls slipped in at eleven beats then by twelve, the dark face of the clock returned to show its bright roman numerals.

In the heavy silence that followed, fleeting thoughts of the unknown terrors I had just escaped from danced before my eyes. I saw my entrails strewn painfully around me and Nimble Nick's gleaming eyes glittering like stars above his jagged and bloody fingers...

The party sighed, murmured, and laughed while the band began once more to play their raging music. It didn't take long for the crowd to fall back into the rhythm of the dance and since there was more space now than ever (and perhaps the partiers were more inebriated) they took up a grand energetic round dance that soon had all the nightmares hooking arms and misshapen limbs into a spiraling, twisting, throbbing throng.

I laughed with silly glee as I was spun between the arms of a spaceman and a howling Banshee. Ahead of me were a couple of laughing clowns wearing masks that made them look like giant birthday cakes. Behind me I saw a creature dressed as a large beetle. They all danced with happy abandon, swaying from side to side and pulling the line this way and that. The Banshee screamed in delight and the beetle behind her gurgled and growled.

When we reached the center of the spiral, we followed the dancing line over and under the merry arms of countless frightful apparitions. Weaving in and out and under and around, I had to remind myself that I was at a party and was safe from all these ghastly frights, so long as I kept my mask on to disguise my identity.

I had worked my way halfway out again when the dance broke up in a jumbled hurdle of laughter in the middle where a tangled mass of limbs writhed for freedom and air. I backed up out of the way so others could lend a hand or claw. I worked my way over to the refreshment table, but the motley mess that lay there was crawling and wiggling so I decided to abstain from drinks or strange foods.

"Not what I would call refreshments either." Said a smooth voice at my shoulder. I looked into the starkly intense eyes of a smooth tall man. He wore a beautiful feathery mask that gave him the impression of a darkly shimmering raven. Beyond the mask, copper red hair curled down his long smooth neck.

"Oh, hi!" I said with a small curtsy.

"Tell me little kitty," He said. "What kind of delicious morsels are you after?"

"Um, I don't know. I'm not hungry. Especially after looking at all that squirming food."

"Ha ha ha!" He laughed deeply. "Don't tell me you don't like to play with your food?"

"Oh, I usually settle for boring old kitty krunchens." I replied

"Well, how bland. I on the other hand love to chase mice just for the sport of it."

"Good thing I'm not a mouse then." I said coyly.

"No, but you could be, would you like to dance?" He stared into my eyes and I felt hypnotized. I wanted to decline but I heard my polite reply instead. He offered me his elbow, which was covered in soft feathers like his mask. The feathers extended to the floor from an elegant coat that was sharply tailored to his long thin frame. His black boots were pointed with little razors on the toes and shiny silver buckles over his high stepping shins.

My vision swarmed with writhing dancing figures as once again I was pulled back into the dance. The band changed its song to a raging chaotic beat and between my swimming head and stumbling feet, I could hardly find the beat. My partner still deftly led me around as if I were but a rag doll in his thin yet strong arms. I felt my body spinning beyond my control, but all I could see where his intense eyes the color of a blue-gray winter sky. He hummed along with the music and I felt my mind empty of childhood memories and future wishes. It was a delirious feeling and as my memories tumbled into his eyes and I saw myself swinging in the park and running through fairy-filled forests as a child, my feet found the rhythm of the dance.

The band played on and on and time seemed to slip away.

A sharp poke in the back and a haughty laugh brought me back to the present and I snapped my eyes closed and shook my head. I looked at my feet and indeed it seemed as if they were floating above the ground, my calico skirt swaying with the spiraling shape of the dance. I cried out in alarm and pushed out of my partner's grip. My feet hit the floor with a thud that shook my jaw and brought my vision to focus.

The dance floor had thinned considerably as many nightmares had departed to other haunts or were taken by the clock. There were many nightmares in disheveled states of intoxication; they had removed their masks to partake of the horrendous treats and drinks and some were passed out in far corners in varied stages of undress. Of those that were still dancing to the cacophony of the band (for the lion bandmaster was no-where to be seen) it seemed each danced to their own rhythm. Three gorillas were waltzing in a lilting circle, the batty hag was fox-trotting with a bloody zombie and the fat King was leading a square dance with a myriad of hosts while the Queen was sulking on her throne smoking from a large pipe that filled the air with noxious smoke.

"What's happened?" I asked as I tried to find my bearings.

"The nights almost over and there are only a few dances left to be had." Said the tall Raven-dressed man with the sky-deep eyes and flashing sharp teeth. "Have you seen the paintings in the upper gallery? They are absolutely breath-taking and worth the little diversion."

"No, I haven't." I replied. "It would be good to take a break from dancing; my head is a little fuzzy."

"Need a breath of fresh air?"

"Perhaps."

"Let me lead the way to the gallery then, it will only take a few moments to see the masterpieces that Dreamworld has to offer." He stuck his elbow in my side and I put my arm through it and followed him to the stairs off the side of the throne. The Queen frowned as we left the dance floor but did not bother to stop us. As I climbed the marble stairs, I could still smell her noxious smoke following us to the upper gallery. A balcony ran around the whole sides of the ballroom and from up there I could see what strange fools were left to saunter and dance around the floor while a monkey played the drums and a hyena played the keyboard.

"Come this way, the paintings are over here."

"Ok." I said and walked to the dim spotlights set upon the huge paintings. I gazed into landscapes of incredible depths, orange and yellow skies met with jagged red and purple mountains where many small men milled about in tedious tasks while giants looked on from above. As I looked, I could see them moving here and there and was reaching out to touch the painting when I was called to view the next. There I saw a hoard of Banshees riding great sea monsters over a raging sea lit by shards of lightning and a crescent moon. The next painting was of a crystal-filled cavern all the crystals glowed with their own sparkling colors of the rainbow and before them was a black demon prancing round a blood red rose bush.

"This one here." Said my host in front of yet another painting. "There is quite a story behind this one I'm sure of it." I came around to look over his shoulder and saw a graveyard filled with fantastical creatures. In one quadrant fairies danced round a big sprawling tree, in another a demon stalked a little girl and her dog and near the top ghosts writhed and rose from their graves with moans upon their tortured lips.

"Look at the details of the trees and each of the graves, you can almost read what some of the markers say on them!" I said. "Oh, and I love the fairies, it makes some weird kind of sense that they would choose to hide in a cemetery. Lots of big trees, and ethereal company…"

"Yes." Said the dark man, "and look how that demon is pouncing for the kill, like a stalking cat." He put his hands on my shoulders and kissed my neck. I felt sharp teeth tease my skin and wiggled out of his grasp to look at the next painting.

A circus scene was depicted with vivid colors so bright the sequins of the ringmaster's jacket sparkled while clowns danced around and elephants paraded, above it all a woman walked a tightrope. I was just starting to comment on this when the great clock rang its loud bell. At the same time, I heard a door open with a loud boom. The roar of several large cats echoed through the suddenly silent hall, their roars ringing over the second and third toll.

"But it's past midnight!" I said to the dark man.

"Here the clock counts to thirteen! Come!" He said and pulled me through the gallery to look over to balcony. The nightmares below were running around in a blind panic as death-filled shadows swept through the hall on the tails of the ice-cold wind. Once they landed on their prey they took form as huge black leopards spewing death from their claws and jaws.

The King and Queen were nowhere to be seen and the masqueraders banged upon bolted doors that led out of the hall. I could see how the entrance to the stairs across from us was blocked off and the nightmares cried in fear as they shook its locked handles.

"Oh, where is Nimble Nick when we need him?" I cried.

"Hush now, we don't want to be noticed."

As the clock continued to toll (and its hands were pointed to the large XIII where a simple I should have been) the panthers fell on their easy prey with the poison of disbelief. They jumped on the nightmares and bit at their throats and tore at their bellies with huge claws. Then they absorbed some of their prey into their shadow bodies, which absorbed all light, color, and flesh that met their deadly fangs and claws. The screaming was terrifying and my dark companion pulled me down below the rail so I could not look upon the desecration below. I pulled at my mask as I covered my ears but he insisted that I keep it on.

That clock seemed to ring forever and the cries continued even after it rang with reverberating silence.

My companion peered over the rail and then pulled me up to look. The disarray was complete. The banquet tables had been thrashed across the floor, giving the crawling entrees a chance for escape while the shadow panthers paced and purred and lay down next to their kills to savor the treats. In a far corner, a group of muddled nightmares huddled in fear. They all clutched their masks tight to their faces as if this alone would keep them safe. The panthers did not seem to notice them until one came rushed up with a large serving platter poised for attack. The panther simply racked him through the middle and he was left sprawling with his entrails falling through his stunned fingers.

"It is the first rule of the Nightmare Masquerade to always wear your mask." Said the dark man. "You will notice that all those that have befallen are without theirs."

What he said was true, the dead Nightmares were all without masks and as I watched, the King timidly opened a side door to let out the survivors. Some of them I recognized as typical nightmare figures. Their awful forms grappled over each other to reach the door in a way I will never forget.

"We should go." I said, as I didn't want to be left in this large hall with only those deathly shadow beasts.

"You are right Oddity." Said the dark man. Around us the walls began to dissolve, their beautiful luster turning into so many glittering ashes.

"I never told you my name!" I exclaimed.

"You didn't have to, I could read it in your eyes."

"And yours?"

"You may call me Draco. And before we leave, I have but one small request."

"And what would that be?" I heard a crash behind him and looked to see a whole section fall under the onslaught of mildew and termites.

"A final kiss."

I submitted to his embrace and gazed into his intense eyes while his mouth covered mine with hard kisses. His eyes were tinged with red and his large black pupils swam in a sea of green. He closed his eyes and then so did I. I then felt him nibbling on my neck and it was such a strange sensation, just a little painful but also, oh so pleasant as my heart beat in time with his dangerous kiss...

The nightmare faded and slowly I woke in my bed, the sheets tangled and sweaty and my neck cocked to the side to make it ache terribly. Yet what really seemed to wake me was the strange and intense thirst I felt. An unquenchable thirst that made me hungry for an uncouth substance that I could not obtain by regular means. It made my throat so sore that I could not speak for weeks. That is why I have written this journal, not told it to you. That and I just can't seem to face the light of day to come over for a visit during reasonable hours...

*Quoted from E.A. Poe, Masque of the Red Death

Passages of my Mind

Come follow me to the darker passages of my mind. I see you cringe in fear of what you'll find, but look past the laughing demons who jump around when finally, you see them. Wipe away the dark smears of fears and wraiths, and let your judgement fly away with the bats. If you make it this far, perhaps you will find the beauty of the darker side. Where secret treasures are revealed to be hidden in our tangled reality.

About Autumn Audosey Augustus

In addition to this short story collection she has written three full length novels which she hopes to successfully publish soon. The Pieces of Pandemonium, The Puzzle of Pandemonium and The Goblin's Wish.

Autumn is the Instigator of Cirkus Pandemonium, a small cirkus troupe that performs many acts of tantalizing thrills. Her skills include aerial silks, trapeze, acro-balance, contact juggling and fire dancing. The Cirkus often performs skits and stories inspired by the fantastic world of Pandemonium and Divine Chaos. In addition, she takes up many hobbies to accomplish her goal of "Do something creative every day!"

Currently Autumn and Cirkus Pandemonium are based in Salt Lake City, Utah, where you may find them cavorting in clubs and festivals.
She is the mother to two beautiful sons, a daughter, a dog, a cat, several fish, and a few thousand bees.

She is a High Priestess of Pan and hopes to instigate inspiration in others through her thoughts and actions. She delights in converting conservatives into a life of magic and mayhem.

Hail Pan! Lord of the dance, the forests, and Divine Chaos!

www.cirkuspandemonium.net www.facebook.com/cirkuspandemonium

Made in the USA
San Bernardino, CA
02 February 2017